Loose

By Patrick Forsyth

With best wishes

Pat Forsyth

© Patrick Forsyth 2017

All rights reserved

Without limiting the rights under copyright reserved above, no part of this publication may be reproduced, stored in or introduced into a retrieval system, or transmitted, in any form or by any means (electronic, mechanical, photocopying, recording or otherwise) without prior written permission of the copyright owner

The right of Patrick Forsyth to be identified as author of this work has been asserted in accordance with sections 77 and 78 of the Copyright, Designs and Patents Act, 1988

This book is a work of fiction. Names, characters, businesses, organisations, places, and events are either the product of the author's imagination or are used fictionally. Any resemblance to actual persons, living or dead, events or locales is entirely coincidental.

This Edition Published by Stanhope Books, Northamptonshire, UK 2017

www.stanhopebooks.com

Cover design and format by Tracy Saunders © 2017

ISBN-13: 978-1-909893-54-2

Dedication: In memory of Sue; whose support of my writing is just one of the things I miss.

Note: The cover design is by artist and graphic designer Tracy Saunders (perhaps best known for her marine paintings) who is, appropriately, resident close to the initial setting of this book.

PRELUDE

Preparations concluded

Certain things need careful preparation.

The scene had to be set just right. In an unremarkable house on the edge of the town, the woman had worked out what was best. She dressed to look professional. A suit, no ostentatious jewellery, just a simple strand of pearls at her neck. Spectacles, well she had to wear them, and anyway she felt doing so hid the expression on her face just a little; her voice was more important. The room had to be just right too. Located near the front door, no tour of the house was necessary to get to it. It was designed to put the focus on her. Just a table and chairs, the table covered with a plain cloth that hung low to the floor, the chairs around the table were upright, but comfortable. The lighting was best low she thought, and on a sideboard she had two candles standing ready to light and set to one side of the table where there were also a couple of bland ornaments; entering a darkened room was not to be recommended though, visitors found it daunting, and so she only drew the curtains as she started her sessions and once her client had been comfortably seated.

Along one wall hung a full length drape of material, dark, almost black but covered in tiny sequins that twinkled in the candle light. A thin thread ran from the corner of the material to her chair so that with a tiny tug she could set the whole wall moving just enough to make the sparkle more noticeable. She wanted no interruptions so she had a switch on her phone to stop it ringing during her work and a neat array of a jug of water and glasses on a tray on the table; if her client coughed or got a dry throat that was easily cured. A box of tissues was secreted in a drawer under the table, allowing easy access in case any tears made them necessary, which sometimes was so. She wanted people to concentrate on her, she wanted a certain formality, a certain strangeness, an atmosphere that seemed appropriate and which matched with the state of mind most usually displayed by her visitors.

Following a brief check to see that the room was set out to her satisfaction, and to place a fresh jug of water on the tray, the woman went through to the kitchen and switched on the kettle. She was ready in good time and could fit in a cup of tea before her next visitor arrived.

These arrangements were not typical of the normal round of events in the small town of Maldon, set on the estuary of the River Blackwater in North Essex. A historic town, home to some of the last traditional sailing barges in the country, and sitting east of the main A12 road that ran north through Chelmsford towards Colchester and beyond, some would describe it as quiet. People of all sorts bustled along the old High Street, or sat chatting in its many coffee shops, but very few of them had experienced what went on in that room.

With these preparations concluded, elsewhere in Maldon another woman was making very untypical preparations of a very different kind, though the two did have one thing in common and, in neither case, could it be described as good.

✤

He knew at once something wasn't right.

He opened the front door as usual, dropped his bag on the floor in the hall, as usual, shrugged off his anorak and dropped it on the floor alongside his bag, also as usual. But he could tell immediately that something was different. Normally when he came home there was activity in the flat, he would be greeted by the sound of a kettle perhaps or dishes clattering in the kitchen, the house would be warm and welcoming and somehow be giving off a familiar air of being occupied.

Today the place was cold, silent and still; it felt unmistakeably empty.

It was very cold in fact, the heating had been on for a while as winter set in, now it felt as if it had not been working all day. He shouted: "Hello. I'm home." But he got no reply. He walked through to the kitchen, a half full mug of tea sat on the side beside the kettle, but it was cold, a grey skin coated its surface. There was no note; normally if anything unusual had happened or if he was coming into an empty flat for some reason there would be an explanatory note secured to the fridge door with a red magnet shaped like an explanation mark and standing out on the white surface. He looked in the living room, went from room to room, there weren't so many, but he found no clue. The whole place was cold, eerily quiet and he shivered, getting a little worried now. What was going on? He got out his mobile phone, made a call, but did not get through; no matter, experience suggested it was unlikely to be switched on.

There must be a simple reason for this he thought, shrugging inwardly, as he got a can of drink from the fridge, clicked on the heating — the button he selected set the boiler whirring to go about its work — and then went into the living room, sat down and put on the television. The air around him slowly warmed. After a couple of hours he was getting hungry, he clicked off the television and the silence returned as the noise of onscreen alien conflict ceased at the touch of a button. He returned to the kitchen and opened the fridge. No meal, no note saying "heat me", awaited him inside, so he rummaged in a cupboard instead and, with judicious use of the microwave, he prepared some baked beans on toast and ate it sitting at the kitchen table a book open beside him. After that he ignored the bowl of apples on the sideboard and ate a bag of crisps and a bar of chocolate, both secreted in a high cupboard, although both hider and seeker knew their location full well.

It was dark outside, in fact it had been beginning to get dark when he got home; he closed the living room curtains, clicked on his mobile phone and made another call. Nothing. He lost himself in the chit chat of social media for a while. Tiring of this he returned to the book he had read while he ate in the kitchen. He had again wondered what to do, but decided just to wait. After all, what else? He shrugged to himself again. Although he stayed up quite late, nothing changed and so finally he went to bed.

Nothing was different in the morning, except that the heating came on as it should and he overslept a little, then having to rush through his morning ritual: bolting down a bowl of cereal, grabbing his bag and heading straight out, still worried but focused on his lateness and resolving to carry on as normal. By the time he got home at the end of the day, he was sure normality would have returned.

✻

Earlier the previous day, just after breakfast, she had given up.

There was just too much that she didn't like and couldn't control. She had no idea what to do and could think of no one and nowhere to turn to. She sat slumped at the kitchen table staring into her mug of cooling tea, and in the near silence a tear ran down her face. The radio played in the corner, the volume low, and she heard it not at all. She got up and, for no reason she could deduce, tidied the kitchen. She washed up everything except her tea mug, there was a little more left in that, opened and closed drawers without quite knowing why and then went out into the small garden at the back of the house. There was still a distinct chill in the air; it had been a cold night. She looked up at the grey sky and wrapped her arms around herself in an instinctive reaction to the chilly air; she had not thought to put on any form of coat. A light wind ruffled her hair. She walked down the short path to where a small timber summer house was positioned in the corner of the little garden, a sign of better times and better weather, a cuppa or a glass of wine sitting at the front of it had been a small pleasure in past years.

She had done all the thinking that she could and resolved only that there was no more to be done. Nothing. She opened the summerhouse door, went inside, pulled it to behind her and sat down on the blue plastic cushion on a wooden garden chair. The single small window was almost obscured by dust and cobwebs, she sat amid the gloom, surrounded by a clutter of garden furniture and the other paraphernalia of the neglected space; a rake toppled over and fell to the floor with a clatter, but she hardly noticed it. She sat there for a long time, her mind blank. It was over, no new way forward came to mind. Soon her whole body was chilled and her exposed hands felt numb. She shivered and fumbled as she felt in the pocket of her apron, she could barely feel her fingers but she managed to retrieve the kitchen knife she had taken from the drawer. Other than making up her mind, that had been the only preparation necessary. Numbed by the cold, she felt very little pain and then quite quickly her mind clouded and, as she drifted away, her last thought was that she had left nothing ready for tea; finally the darkness was total.

During the day the weather outside continued to be wintery, a cold snap making the temperature lower than one would expect for the time of year. It was dank, dreary and cold. Later, when he came home, he would have no reason to go out into the garden, no reason at all.

CHAPTER ONE

A bit of a problem

Philip Marchington had a problem. He was trying to turn his mind to a domestic matter about which he had the germ of an idea, but which demanded his best possible response. But he was at work: recently he had been put in charge of the town library in Maldon and he took his new role very seriously. He loved his job, but today it was proving difficult to concentrate; his mind wanted to be elsewhere. Almost as soon as he arrived there had been various encounters with library users. He liked meeting his regular members, but sometimes people expected, well, what they expected just surprised him. Currently he was at the library front desk and faced by a woman demanding his undivided attention. She had approached immediately Philip had started his stint at the desk, saying "good morning" with a smile and then posing her question. She appeared to be somewhere in her early forties, wearing a cosy blue anorak and a slightly distracted expression. He didn't remember seeing her before, but that was good, he wanted to see as many new library users as possible. She could be a future regular.

"Do you have a book about careers for young people? I'm trying to get my daughter to think ahead." As she put the question she made it sound like a bit of a chore. Philip imagined a surly teenager at home not wanting to know about such things.

It was a routine question and thus unlike some of those posed that bordered on the bizarre. Already earlier in the morning he had been asked where the "fictional novels" were located, been castigated and promised hellfire and brimstone for having books by Richard Dawkins on the shelves and been told off because he had not read one particular book beloved by the enquirer, who evidently felt that any proper librarian should be a sufficiently voracious reader to consume the contents of his entire library. Philip loved reading but there were only so many books he could get through. This enquiry sounded more sensible and serious and he responded in kind.

"There are a good number of career guides in the reference section." Philip pointed across the open plan space to a shelf nearby. "Do you want something about any particular area of work?"

"No, no she has no idea yet," the woman replied turning her eyes down to her side and continuing "stay there a second Julia and I'll go and look."

Philip then noticed a small child of perhaps five or six years of age standing below the counter clutching a teddy bear. She smiled up at him.

"Hello, Julia," he offered as she smiled up at him. "Do you know what you want to be when you grow up?"

"Oh yes" she replied, a confident smile widening across her entire face. "I shall be a dragon trainer." She said it with complete certainty.

Philip chuckled as Julia turned towards her mother as she headed back from the reference section holding a book; she seemed to have found one she considered suitable and, given that her reply had indicated that she was already into books, Philip wondered if she and her daughter would become regular library users. Certainly it seemed likely that a little more research would be necessary before the career selection dilemma was definitively solved. After they left he continued through what became a busy day, a day with one odder event in store: he found a mysterious unexplained card on the library notice board.

✵

Elsewhere in the town another of his library regulars was finding that she had a bit of a problem. Mary Donaldson's husband had died three months ago, but here she was sitting comfortably at a table in a candle lit living room all ready to speak to him.

"Quiet now Mary, we're getting close now, very close, I'm sure George is within reach."

Mary had been persuaded to contact a psychic by a well-meaning friend worried about how hard she had taken her husband's death. It had been sudden. He had had a stroke, dying in his sleep so that Mary had suffered the trauma of trying to rouse him when she woke and found him unmoving beside her in the morning. Unsurprisingly she had been confused and unsure what was going on, but she remembered sitting on the side of the bed phoning for an ambulance. While she waited for it to arrive, the awful truth dawned. He was only fifty seven.

"He's close, he's close," the psychic's voice interrupted her thoughts as it took on a clear, but whispered urgency.

She was called Jane Wearing, a homely looking woman, slightly plump, smartly dressed but with unruly greying hair the arrangement of which Mary thought had to be an experiment unsuitable to be repeated, and horned rimmed spectacles that appeared to be a size too large for her face. She had been so sensitive with Mary when they had first met, talking about both the process of grief and about Mary's husband; a subject Mary found she was happy to talk about at length. She asked a great many questions and the session had been over in what seemed like moments, though it had lasted a full hour. Mary paid her the fifty pounds due and left with reassurances that contact would soon be possible, that her mind would then be put at rest and that she would be enabled to move on with her life. Her new life Mary had thought, it was certain things were not ever going to be the same. Although she had no firm belief in an afterlife, she found it odd that the encounters brought some comfort and were also unaccountably moreish. She found herself arranging another session.

But nothing happened at the next session, or the next, or indeed the fourth. No contact, just talk, soothing comments and bland assurances about the future. Mary found her sadness and disappointment turning to suspicion. Her rational side told her this was all nonsense and that she was being taken for a fool. But maybe... despite her reservations she had found that hope had overpowered common sense and she had resolved to have one more session. And here she was with contact now being well-nigh promised.

Jane Wearing's voice deepened a little.

"Hello, darling" she said, her figure unmoving, then in her normal voice, "It's George, it's your George". She went on, her voice deeper again, "I don't want you to be so sad Mary, I'm fine, you have to start to get out and live life again. You should have a holiday, you should go somewhere new, somewhere exotic, perhaps to India."

Mary knew it was not George's voice and she knew too, in that moment, that there was no way it could be his words either. She hated Indian food, always had, even the smell turned her stomach and knowing this, George would never, ever have suggested India as an ideal holiday destination. She did remember telling Jane about their joint love of travel however, she had mentioned places they had been and liked: Australia, New Zealand, and California amongst others – she had fond memories of some splendid trips they had taken together. She was sure, she stood up in a sudden rush jogging the table and making the teacups rattle. She had been so stupid she now realised and as a cold rage gripped her, Jane Wearing looked shocked and opened her mouth to speak, but Mary was ahead of her.

"You're a fake," she leant forward a little and spoke through gritted teeth. "My George would never have suggested that, he knows full well…" she paused, becoming business-like despite her emotional feelings, "… no, I won't even talk about it, I now know you're just a cynical fraud and I want nothing more to do with you."

Before the so-called psychic could react Mary was on her feet, had turned on her heel and stormed out of the house, grabbing her coat from the banister in the hall as she went. She gave the front door a satisfying slam behind her. She felt silly, she felt used and, it also occurred to her, she felt a significant bit poorer too, though she had left without paying for this last session. She felt that fact offered a tiny victory. She pulled on her coat, walked a few yards then stopped a little way down the road, opened her handbag to get out a tissue and mopped the tears that were staining her cheeks, but she resolved there and then not to let the matter rest. Somehow she would put a stop to the wretched woman's activity if it was the last thing she did.

Inside the house, Jane Wearing wrote off her vanishing client to experience, she'd had great hopes for Mary but reflected that you can't win them all, though her little side line had successfully clocked up payment for several sessions before Mary had taken against her. There would be others, indeed, if she had really been able to foretell the future as she also claimed, she would have known not only that there would be a new one before too long but how their visit would turn out.

✢

Philip Marchington turned into his street having walked home from the library, which was situated behind the shops at the top end of Maldon's High Street. As he drew near to the house he saw lights on inside; for a moment he found himself surprised by the fact. In the years since the death of his wife, Penny, he had grown used to always going back into an empty house after work. But recently all that had changed.

The recent death of his friend and near neighbour, Abigail Croft, had somehow led him into tracking down her long lost son Michael, without whose location her estate would have reverted to the government. He had discovered that, following a family row, Michael had gone to Singapore and then to Thailand and, although the trail was some twenty years old, he had ended up taking a trip there and, perhaps against all the odds, finding Michael in a marina on the island of Phuket, living happily and busy working with his beloved sailing boats. Sadly a misunderstanding and a lost letter when he had first arrived there meant that he and his mother had become estranged and had never had any contact again. As he began to investigate the situation he had met Miriam, Sergeant Jayne of the local Maldon police, she had become involved in assisting his search and, as they began to become close, she had accompanied him on his exploratory trip to Phuket. As his research had led to a successful conclusion, they had enjoyed a great holiday.

Rather to his amazement he had proposed to her and now, she having moved out of her small flat, Miriam and he were living together… so the lights in the house being on should be no surprise to him: tonight it seemed that she was home before him. Philip's work at the Library involved working shifts, and Miriam's police work certainly did, so they both kept less than regular hours.

"Hello. Anyone home?" Philip called out as he entered the hall, hung his satchel on a hook and returned his keys to his pocket. Absurd he thought as he said the words, clearly there was someone home and clearly it had to be Miriam.

"Miriam?" he added.

"I'm in here," her voice came from the kitchen.

He went through and they kissed. Miriam was still in her police uniform and his kissing an officer of the law had fast become a running joke between them. So he added "With your permission Ma'am" and they both grinned.

It is surprising how quickly habits form in a new relationship. They always spent a moment with the "How was your day?" question and liked to hear what each other had been up to, though Miriam was reticent about speaking of some of the things her work involved. Sometimes this was because she felt that what her work involved was routine and uninteresting, sometimes it was because she did not want Philip to worry for her; there could be an unpleasant side to police work too.

"Good day for me" said Philip in reply to Miriam's query as he sat down at the kitchen table while Miriam continued busying herself with preparing the supper.

It had not been so long since he took over as head of the library, his old boss, the ultra-officious Miss Frobisher, having been moved out by the powers that be; she was not a book lover and her plans to turn the library into some sort of high tech hub of the community were so over the top that she had run foul of officialdom and been moved to what Philip called "some bean-counting job in a book-free zone". To preserve his vision of how the library should be he had, he admitted, encouraged her a little towards her demise and was now relishing his new position; he felt the library, and its patrons were the better for the change. He had a job he loved back on track, a new lady in his life after the difficulties and sadness of his wife's illness and death, and most recently a wedding to arrange too.

"Remember me telling you about Terry Walsh?" he asked, not pausing for an answer. "Well today …"

Terry Walsh was a library regular. He was always a voracious reader and his mother had brought him in at least once a week when he was young. Now aged about thirteen or fourteen years old Philip guessed, he was a gangling lad and Philip usually saw him in school uniform as he came in once school was finished, usually with a bulging knapsack, his shirt hanging out and his tie removed or askew. He always had a word with Philip, who saw encouraging young people to read as an important part of his duties and had long engaged him in conversation. He asked for recommendations, checking what titles were like and asking too for something else "like this" as he handed one book back and went about selecting another.

Today Philip had come across him sitting at a table, an unusual occurrence, and with his mother nowhere to be seen. He had a thick Harry Potter novel at his elbow. He had read the last wizard novel a while back and he was on the most recent volume now, the one in the form of a play, and also had a thick computer tome that looked to be too serious for light reading. It tied in with what Terry referred to as "the project"; something he had to do for school and which demanded that he set out what it should be. But he was looking at something else and he had shut that book in front of him with a snap as Philip had spoken to him. It seemed clear he did not want Philip to see what it was.

"I wonder if that's the last chapter, eh, Terry," he said, nodding at the Harry Potter and adding, "On your own today – how's your mother? I've not seen her in here for a little while."

"She's fine." Terry seemed somewhat no-committal but went on without pause, putting his hand on the Harry Potter book, "yes, last one, though this has come a while after the original last one, so who knows... anyway, I must go."

Philip wished him well and watched as Terry got up and went on his way. He collected up his school bag and went to the desk to check out his new book. But he went via a shelf to which he returned the reference book he had been consulting to its designated place. He hoped that Mr M, as he always called Philip, hadn't noticed.

Philip told Miriam about the encounter.

"The odd thing was I've never seen him sitting reading like that before and, although he tried to hide it and I didn't comment, I couldn't help noticing that the book he was looking at was about adoption. Seemed rather odd."

Miriam paused in her cooking and asked Philip if he could lay the table, he rose and began to do so as she continued:

"Maybe he's adopted, he's about the age when he might want to find out about it if he is, isn't he?"

"Maybe. I don't know, though his father left when he was little. It's probably nothing. I'll only worry if he's checking out a book on brain surgery next time."

"What about you?" Philip asked Miriam. She still felt her work was too routine and too lacking in interest to catalogue much for him, though it had its moments, including some difficult to talk about, and today, well, there had been one rather odd incident. But not now she thought, her mind engaged on grilling sausages.

"Nothing special" she said, "although we were summoned to a domestic incident at one point. That can sometimes be nasty and the incidence of domestic violence locally is increasing too, I'm not sure why, it's often drink related. Anyway this time the main complaint seemed to be an argument about the television: the woman who came to the door saying 'He won't let me watch BBC 1'. That was it, nothing more, no violence; the things that prompt some people to dial 999, really, sometimes I wonder! Come on, supper's ready now and don't we need to talk about arrangements for a certain wedding?"

Philip smiled. In their different ways they both got some pretty inappropriate questions asked of them at work.

"Right. Much more interesting," he said as they sat down at the table. The conversation went to and fro across the table. What sort of wedding should it be? Should it be sooner or later, should it be a small or large event? On this last they agreed: they both wanted it small, neither wanted any sort of fuss – but nothing was finally decided and Philip wanted it to be right, he wanted Miriam to enjoy it. He had turned his mind to the problem a dozen times during the day, but a hectic day in the library had prevented him from having more than the germ of an idea. He knew he had to give the whole thing more thought.

"I think I might have one idea" he told her "but it's getting late, I want to check something out about it first, more anon, okay?"

"Fine," said Miriam. "As long as you don't change your mind about the whole thing. I'll leave it with you for the moment, but I do expect it to be dealt with as a priority, you know!"

"Well, I certainly don't propose changing my mind and it *is* a priority" said Philip smiling, they still teased each other about the speed with which they had got together and, despite his delight at all that had happened, Philip still found his head remained in a bit of a whirl about it all. Soon after they got back from Thailand having found Abigail's long lost son, they had gone to visit Philip's sister and family who lived a little more than an hour away. She had been very good to him after his wife Penny had died and regularly asked him down to her home in Kent for a meal with the family, often Sunday lunch, always saying meaningfully "do bring a friend if you want". He had known what she implied and had come to hate the comment, yet recognised that she only wanted what was best for him. Then he had gone from a regular polite ignoring of his sister's suggestions to saying that he would in fact bring someone this time, then refusing all enquiries, and arriving on the day and introducing Miriam as "the lady I'm going to marry". His sister's face was a picture. He had very much enjoyed the moment, his only regret being that Miriam was not dressed in her uniform and that they had not arrived in a police car with a siren wailing and blue lights flashing. He had visions of the children's reaction to that. Miriam got the fullest approval from all the family and that had pleased him no end.

"There was another odd thing today" he said, returning to the review of the day. "We have a notice board in the library, you know to post news of local events and especially for anything linked to books." Miriam nodded. "Well, I found this on it today."

He felt in his pocket and produced a yellow, postcard-sized note on which was typed in large capitals: THE COUNTDOWN BEGINS … There was a pin hole through the top and the day's date was in the bottom left hand corner.

"People are supposed to ask if something can be put up there, we don't usually get anything, well, just appearing." He remembered the definitely not missed Miss Frobisher having some rooted objection to almost anything that a member might request be displayed. She once even found a notice about a proposed poetry reading event "too commercial" on the basis that a participant might actually sell a book of their poetry at the event; what an idea. While space was limited, and priority had to be given to library related matters, Philip was happy to see the board packed with information.

"What do you think it means?" Philip continued.

"Whatever it is I think you should expect to get some more," Miriam replied as she served up their food and placed a plate in front of him.

"Thanks. How so?" said Philip, still thinking as much about how it had appeared there as what it might mean.

"Well it's a countdown isn't it, maybe you'll have another one every day until the world ends." She giggled. Philip smiled too, but nevertheless he still thought it was odd. He thanked Miriam again for her cooking and they tucked into the meal.

CHAPTER TWO

That awful woman

"No, no, stop." The woman shouting in a shrill voice held up her arms for protection in front of her.

Miriam enjoyed her work as a police Sergeant but she was the first to admit that a good deal of it was routine. There was also a lot of form filling with that punctuated by occasionally danger or sadness; she sometimes felt she would never really get used to picking up the pieces after a road accident, though she felt she acquitted herself pretty well on such an occasion. Only the other day she had attended a smash – what they referred to as a road traffic accident or RTA -where a speeding driver had hit another car while taking a bend too fast on the narrow Goldhanger Road, one of those leading away from the town. The man, who, when tested, had proved to be over the alcohol limit, had hit the other vehicle obliquely and run on finally coming to a halt on the grass verge. His car was damaged but he was little more than shaken. His victim had not been so lucky, she was alive, but swerving trying to avoid or minimise the collision had sent her into a ditch and given her injuries that might well scar her for life. Miriam found the fact that such a thing was entirely unnecessary irked her and made it more difficult to deal with without being upset herself.

On other occasions she was involved in quirky one off incidents and one such occurred today. This time she had been called to a house on the outskirts of Maldon where a neighbour had reported vandalism taking place. She pulled up at the kerb expecting to see a young man, most often with vandalism the culprit was a young man, instead she found a respectable woman in early middle age spray painting a garage door; the words "fake and fraud" stood out in bright red letters. Outside the front door a woman, who looked slightly older and equally respectable, stood shouting for the first one to stop, though she was keeping her distance. A diagonal stripe of red paint ran across her body from shoulder to waist. As she drew up Miriam pressed a switch to give a single burst on the siren, and the sudden loud noise made both women turn towards her. The sprayer let the hand holding the spray drop to her side.

"Enough. Enough. Stop it. Stop it now." Miriam shouted and both women stood motionless turned towards her as she exited the car. She went forward with her arm extended adding "Give me that can. Now". The first woman did not do so but instead she let it drop to the ground.

"She deserves it," she said. "She deserves this and more".

"What on earth is all this about?" Miriam asked looking at the woman whose house had been defaced.

"She attacked me, she's ruined a good suit," the householder spluttered.

"I can see that, now: what's your name?" asked Miriam getting out a notebook and adopting an official tone. She knew that launching into the procedural matters could distance people from whatever had been going on. The woman took a step back so that her front door was only a couple of feet behind her. She looked fearful, more so now than when she was under attack.

"Just leave me alone and get that, that... person away from me," she spluttered.

"If we are going to sort it out I will need some details," Miriam responded, but the woman just shook her head and stepped back into the house.

"I don't want to press charges, just make her go away." She spoke from the doorway, turned and stepped inside - and then slammed her front door behind her so hard that the brass knocker adorning it knocked twice.

"What about you? What's your name?" she turned to the paint sprayer who was sitting to one side on the garden wall sobbing soundlessly. There was a slight hesitation as the woman perhaps wondered at the wisdom of giving her name, then she spoke.

"I'm Mary Donaldson. But she's not pressing charges, can't we just leave it?" she managed, looking mortified now the adrenalin rush had subsided. "It's silly, I was silly too, no real harm was done but she's, she's... no, I'd rather not talk about it. Please." A moment ago she had seemed about to lay into her opponent again, instead she now held a handkerchief to her nose, hung her head and added: "I'm sorry."

Miriam took her address. She wondered what it was about but saw little merit in prolonging the exchange, the paint sprayer seemed honestly contrite and it did not seem likely that the confrontation would continue. Miriam continued with a question. "Do you have a car here?" she looked at the street lined with a good number of parked vehicles and the woman nodded.

"Well, I suggest you go home and think about other ways of dealing with whatever this 'silly thing' is."

"Right, I will, thank you … and I'm sorry. I just didn't know what else to do."

Miriam hesitated, curious, she wondered if she should discover more or take more formal action, after all physical damage had been done, but at that moment her radio crackled into life. She excused herself and had a brief conversation with HQ. She was wanted elsewhere.

"Okay we'll leave it there, I can contact you again if necessary, and this call sounds urgent." She walked back to the police car, watching as the woman picked up the spray can, put it into a plastic bag she retrieved from her coat pocket and walked to her car and drove away as she set off in the opposite direction. But she did wonder what it had all been about.

While Miriam was busy with her paint spray lady, Philip was busy at the library. He had found a second countdown note on the library notice board. The printed words read: A DEADLINE

NEEDED. BE READY… and it was in the same form as before, a yellow card pinned to the notice board. Still mystified as to what they referred to, he took it down and put it in his desk drawer with the first one, making a note to ask his colleagues about it at the next staff meeting.

He then took a moment to check his personal email. He was expecting a message from Abigail's son Michael Croft in Phuket and found it was there waiting. He and Michael had been corresponding about Michael's impending visit to sort out his mother's house. With a visit to Maldon imminent, Philip had posed him another question about an idea he'd had, and hoped for a comment about that. The incoming message was simple:

Yes, it can be done. In fact it's no problem, I can make all the arrangements locally (while you look after Mum's house!). I'll check dates for the UK visit with you very soon. Best regards … Mac. P.S. Poy says hello.

Both he and Miriam were looking forward to the visit. Having found Michael, Mac as he liked to be called, and met his Thai partner Poy, who was clearly a prime reason for him having stayed and made his life in Thailand, they had all got on well and Philip looked forward to seeing them again and to seeing Abigail's affairs all finally settled. He had promised to give Mac a hand, after all he had not been in the U.K. for more than twenty years and some of the things to be seen to would otherwise have to be done, with difficulty, from across the world.

Just then Margaret, the youngest of the Library's team, came up to take over at the desk from him. She was a bright girl and Philip had high hopes for her; he was planning to give her more responsibility.

"My turn," she said. "And …" she hesitated and Philip looked at her waiting to see what came next, as a question seemed about to be posed. She decided to speak.

"I didn't quite know what to do, there's a lady sitting in the corner. She's been there a while and she's crying. Over there." She pointed.

"Okay," Philip sighed "You take over here and I'll go and have a word."

At one of the tables on the far side of the Library, an area used by library members to read both magazines and newspapers as well as books, a woman sat, head bowed, tissue in hand, snuffling. He recognised her as a regular – Mary Donaldson - she usually read the likes of Joanna Trollope and crime novels as he recalled – but she normally seemed a cheerful soul and always said hello. He walked across to her.

"Hello there. Are you alright?" Philip asked and, getting no reply, added "Anything I can do to help? That book can't be that bad." He pointed to a book lying on the table in front of her and tried to inject a jocular tone into his speech, but she just gave a sob. Over the years Philip had found that certain people regarded the Library as a refuge. Some came in to escape the cold, while away time or avoid something in the world outside. Others wanted someone to talk to, and he had regularly found himself involved in conversations ranging from the traumas of marriage break up to the design of a perpetual motion machine and patent law. The machine was clearly only a pipe dream and he had heard no more about it, but Philip had always been clear, you could not ignore this sort of thing; he sat down next to her.

"Mrs Donaldson isn't it?" She looked up, dabbed her face with the tissue she had been clutching in her hand, and replied, her voice a little unsteady.

"Mary. It's Mary. I've been so silly," she said, apparently succeeding in pulling herself together a little as she spoke.

"Do you want to tell me about it?" Philip knew that sometimes just talking about things could help, besides it might turn out to be something simple. He hoped so. He moved round to be opposite her and she visibly pulled herself together a little.

"I sprayed her with paint," Mary Donaldson said in a whisper. It was not at all the sort of comment he had expected.

"You what? Sprayed who?"

"That awful woman. The police came. A woman, a sergeant I think. I felt too silly to tell her what she'd done. But anyway then her radio went off, she was wanted for something else I think, something urgent she said and as that woman didn't want to press charges it was left there."

Philip guessed he knew the sergeant. "What had she done?" He asked, realising as he said it that any explanation would probably take a while; he doubted that Mary had sprayed paint at someone, however awful they might be, merely on a whim. For a while Mary said nothing, apparently considering whether to speak at all. Just as the pause looked as if it might give them time to read an entire novel, it all came out: first the death of Mary's husband, the shock, her grief, then her friend introducing her to the psychic, then the meetings she had attended with Jane Wearing and the subsequent paint spraying incident after she had stormed out of the last one.

"She was a fake of course, what else? How could I have been so silly?" She said, "And it's not just upsetting, the woman is a con artist, I paid her £50 a session. Money for nothing. Once I came to my senses I wanted to frighten her, and I wanted to stop her from doing it to someone else. I went back – with the paint." Her face now showed less upset and more determination.

"You are certainly not silly. You were grieving. You still are. Now, do I understand right, are you saying the policewoman didn't find out what it was all about?"

"No," she replied. "I was frankly too embarrassed to say any more. Now perhaps I wish I had."

"Well, maybe I can help …" Philip hesitated slightly, wondering what he was letting himself in for, as Mary looked suddenly apprehensive. He went on "… just informally I mean," he continued. "You see I think I know the police Sergeant, Sergeant Jayne, in fact I know her rather well. We're engaged!" He smiled both to encourage Mary and because he still smiled at even the thought of Miriam. "Let me tell her about this, I'm sure she will remember your paint spraying, and then we'll see what can be done. I know Miriam will take it seriously. And be sensitive about it too."

"I don't want to get into any trouble. I realise I should not have retaliated as I did… but maybe, informally as you say, yes okay. I don't want her to get away with it. She hurts people."

"She certainly seems to, let me have her name and address would you? Don't worry about it now and we'll have a word again next time you come in. Give me a while, by the time you've finished that next book I may have some news."

"Okay, thank you so much."

After Mary had gone on her way, clearly feeling better for the exchange, Philip pocketed the paper on which she had written a name and address and went back about his work. He was running late now and had a reading to do at a local school in the afternoon. He told Margaret he was going out on a school visit and went on his way. Such visits were now more difficult to accommodate given his new responsibilities and he wondered if Margaret could help with that in future.

At home that evening he broached the subject of the paint spraying incident with Miriam.

"Did you find yourself dealing with a middle aged woman spray painting someone the other day?"

"Well, yes, but how do you know about that? It didn't go anywhere, the lady who was sprayed beat a hasty retreat inside saying she didn't want to take it any further and then I was summoned elsewhere, so I never found out what it was all about. Don't tell me she moved on to spray the Library."

"No, nothing like that, the sprayer's name is Mary Donaldson and she was very upset. I found her this morning sitting crying at one of the tables in the Library. I know her slightly, she's a regular. It took me a little while to calm her down and I promised to talk to you about it."

"So what was it all about? It seemed odd: two apparently respectable ladies in such a situation. I'd have found out more if the radio hadn't summoned me."

"Mary felt she had been conned." Philip told Miriam about what had happened, stressing how a grieving Mary had been upset and had paid out money she now felt was for nothing.

"She's right too," he finished. "The woman is clearly a fraud and although the encouragement towards a next session may not be hard sell, she is conning people."

"Oh dear," said Miriam. "This is such a difficult kind of thing. It sounds dreadful, and I'm sure it should be simple to do something about it, but I can tell you it's not. Mary went there voluntarily, after all, several times, just describing what happened to her isn't likely to be considered as evidence. Whatever she said about the woman it would doubtless be denied."

"Do you mean by that that there is nothing that can be done about it?"

"Well, Mary could make a complaint of course, but frankly I can't see it going anywhere."

"It seems a shame. This woman clearly appears to be a charlatan, she's promising contact with the dead, for goodness sake, telling fortunes and I don't know what else. Yet you say nothing can be done. So other people will doubtless be upset in future just as Mary was, and be out of pocket too." Philip's voice rose a little as he emphasised how strongly he felt. He could not but think how he had felt after the death of his wife, surely he wouldn't have been drawn into anything like this as Mary had been, but nevertheless it was a nasty thought.

"Well, by all means tell her she can make a complaint. That alone might make her feel better; but I can't promise anything."

The conversation then turned to other things, but privately Philip resolved to think on it further. He felt it was an unsatisfactory situation and felt too that maybe, just maybe, something could be done about it. He found he had the first glimmerings of an idea.

*

As they spoke Terry Walsh was back at home wondering what to eat for supper. He liked Philip Marchington, trusted him, but, although he had told him his mother was fine, the truth was he had not seen her for enough days to worry him. He had come home from school one day and she was gone, no note, no nothing ... and he had not heard a word from her since. He was used to her erratic behaviour, and she would sometimes disappear for a while without explanation, but never overnight and she was almost always at home when he returned from school, or if not there was a note. This was different. It had been so long. He had no idea what had happened, he rather assumed whatever it was it was because she had no job — she had lost her job at one of the shops in the High Street and she had told him she was "depressed". He was not sure what that meant exactly, she seemed fine sometimes, then she would spend days at a time shut away in her bedroom. He had kind of got used to that, it was just how things were. He had told no one of her disappearance, said nothing at school, and now things were getting difficult, not least because there was very little food left in the house. At first, he had just assumed she would be back any minute, so there was no need to say anything, then, as time went by, the moment to speak out seemed to have passed and he felt that if he now said anything he might get into trouble for saying nothing sooner. Now, though in many ways he still expected her to walk back into the house at any moment, he was beginning to feel that the circumstances meant that maybe he would have to tell someone. But who?

CHAPTER THREE

More than just a ferry

Thousands of miles away from the small Essex town of Maldon on a sailing boat on the Andaman Sea off the coast of the Thai island of Phuket a question was posed.

"Why are we stopping?" the passenger looked around and added "is anything wrong?"

"No, just changing course a little, soon be there now."

At the helm Abigail Croft's son Michael, Mac to all his friends, had been enjoying the sail. The conditions were ideal, ample wind but not too choppy, the boat soared along and the voyage to the island had been exhilarating. It was a feeling of which he felt he would never tire. His beloved boat "Footloose" had carried the middle-aged Chinese couple for an island picnic. They had apparently enjoyed it all very much, wading ashore when the boat dropped anchor, walking along the beautiful, unspoilt beach and tucking into the elaborate meal Poy, Michael's Thai partner, had prepared and brought ashore, but they had shown no interest in the boat at all. Usually Michael would be demonstrating things about the boat's sailing characteristics to his passengers, letting them take the helm and often there was a real instructional element to the trips he made. The boat was a beauty, forty plus feet of teak decked perfection in Mac's view; it was now not in the first flush of youth perhaps, but it remained Mac's pride and joy. On this sail he had recognised early on that their passengers were only interested in the outing and he had just enjoyed himself. Their virtual stop was only because he had been taking advantage of the wind, tacking to and fro with the boat heeling over a little and spray coming up from the bow and blowing away in the breeze, water droplets sparkling in the bright sunlight. Now he had slowed, gone about, and turned the boat onto a new course aiming back towards the marina on Phuket. For a moment the boat was almost stationary before the wind filled the sails again and "Footloose" moved ahead.

Michael had met Poy when he had first arrived in Phuket, having been hired to help its owner sail "Footloose" from Singapore to the island and deliver it to a local buyer. When the sale had fallen through, then she had been a prime influence in persuading him to buy the boat and set up chartering it as a business. When romance quickly blossomed she had become his life partner as well as a business one and they had operated the business together very happily ever since. They did not make a fortune, but enjoyed their way of life enormously. For Michael it was a dream come true; he had never wanted to do anything but sail, it was a choice that had led to some acrimony with his parents when he might have gone to university as they had wanted. Instead he had taken the boat moving job and gone off to the east in something of a huff. As misunderstanding and distance compounded the problem when he had first arrived on the island of Phuket, he had soon lost all touch; though he had inherited money when out of the blue his father died that had enabled him to buy "Footloose". Years later also out of the blue Philip Marchington had made contact with him, following up tenuous clues and tracking him down on a visit to the island, and he now had his late mother's estate to see to; indeed Philip was helping in England, a task that included setting things up for her house to be sold.

"How long landfall?"

Poy's head appeared in the entrance to the cabin as she asked the question in the sing-song accent affected by many Thais when they speak English. Twenty years living with Michael had done little to alter the sound, though her vocabulary had extended since they met and was now extensive. She clambered up and sat beside him as he held the helm. Michael smiled as she joined him. She can handle the boat as well as I can he mused and she still looks as stunning as she did the first time we sailed to one of the islands just after we met. He had an abiding image in his mind from that day of her stripping off her shirt and shorts and diving over the side looking wonderful in a bikini. He had been smitten there and then, more so as they got to know each other.

"Maybe forty five minutes," he said, adding for the sake of his passengers "we're nearly there, you should get reception soon." The man had taken out a mobile phone and was holding it up and looking at the signal strength indicator. As it would not work yet, he put it back in his pocket and talked quietly with his wife as the distance to the shore became less and less.

"You cannot put it off more." Poy said as she sat down beside him in the cockpit. Michael knew what she meant: they had to go to England and check out his mother's house. He knew he could not sell it without seeing it and checking the contents too, there were bound to be some loose ends.

"It's not easy," he replied. "I just feel it's such a risk to leave 'Footloose' here unattended."

"Not risk, excuse," Poy replied at once. "You must see to mother's house and finish it; it's honourable thing."

"I know, I know," he said "But I'm still not comfortable with being away; perhaps I need an assistant, someone to look after the boat during the trip to England."

Poy was quick to answer: "You *have* assistant!" she said. "Or do you forget me?" She gave his arm a playful punch.

"Then you can take care of the boat, carry on the business," he said.

"No, no, decided already," she said. "I come with you to England. Your mother give you money, house, business can wait a little while. Besides I have arranged babysitter for boat. Pia can do, watch every day, no problem." Pia worked in an office on the marina at which they moored, one of many there concerned with boats and boating, she helped take bookings for them, she was a friend and they both knew her well.

Michael knew there was no easy way out of that, he too trusted Pia completely. He also knew the settling up in England must be done. He glanced at the Chinese couple. The man got a connection on his phone as he watched and soon became taken up with a phone conversation; his wife seemed happy enough watching the sea rush by. She met his gaze and smiled. He turned back to Poy.

"Okay, I know you're right. I had an email from Philip suggesting some dates when we might visit. We would need to be away for a couple of weeks. I guess."

"Three, three better, I can see England, I can see where you lived."

"Well ..."

"It agreed. Okay, now I'll take her in." Poy nudged Michael aside and he moved over to let her take the helm as the entrance to the marina came close.

"Philip wrote about something else too," said Michael as Poy navigated with care and precision into the marina and he went forward to drop the sails so that they could hold direction and motor into their allotted berth. "He wants our help."

"How help?"

"I'll show you the email," replied Michael. "Anyway I think it's more your department than mine, let's talk about it later." He moved forward and jumped onto the pontoon to secure the boat as Poy expertly brought them alongside with barely a bump.

Once the boat was stable and unmoving he escorted his passengers up the steps to the marina, took their payment for the trip and expressed the hope that they had enjoyed themselves. At this point they seemed to take an interest and made their pleasure in being taken to what they described as seeming like "our own private island" clear, and declared that they had enjoyed a "very satisfactory trip".

"They seem happy enough" he told Poy back on board, "but our boat was wasted on those two, I think. Really, I like to think we are more than just a ferry."

They stowed equipment, tidied the whole boat and collected and bagged up the remains of the picnic then, having been out for most of the day, Michael led them towards the hotel that formed a part of the marina complex; an hour there by the pool to relax seemed like a suitable plan. He had long ago made an arrangement with the hotel to use it in this way. They both swam for a while then, as they sat at a table alongside the pool, cold drinks in front of them, drying off, they saw a sizable lizard alongside the pool, four feet or more in length. It lay unmoving in the sun. An American woman, in all likelihood a guest in the hotel, holding hands with a small child passed close by and saw the lizard too: she stopped dead in her tracks in front of it. She took a step back, looking aghast and turning to them as the nearest people asked: "Is that alright?"

Her tone was urgent, worried and somewhat strident making her American accent sound harsh. Poy gave her a broad smile.

"Oh, yes," she replied. "Is very happy, just sunning itself."

She grinned at Michael. She knew full well what the woman had meant and reassured her when she asked, in a less ambiguous way now, if the creature was dangerous.

"No, doesn't bite, Madam" she said still smiling.

The woman hurried away with a quick "thanks" and chose loungers at the far end of the pool well away from what she appeared to be convinced was a dangerous monster. Michael returned Poy's grin, but told her not to tease the tourists.

"I needed this drink, I guess we seem to have an overseas trip to fix."

"And what else? What for Philip?" Poy asked.

"Later" replied Michael, "holiday stuff. The priority now is beer, though it looks like we will see Philip and Miriam here in Thailand again, they loved their last visit." With that he drained his glass, turned to an approaching waitress and ordered two more cold *Singha* beers. But he knew they would talk more about visiting England soon and he knew also that he would fix to go; no more delays. He knew Poy, as was so often the case, was right. It had to be done, and it should be done soon.

✽

The following day some two hundred kilometres or so away in Bangkok, the voice speaking into the telephone was soft, but clear, professional and authoritative.

"It will be done, no problem, I will email you all details later this afternoon."

Khun Katai rang off and put the note she had written herself as she had spoken on the telephone on one side and picked up the telephone again; something needed sorting out and she was the person to fix it. The Oriental Hotel had long had an iconic presence in the city of Bangkok: since 1876, or perhaps earlier, the exact date being unclear, the hotel had sat a serene presence on the banks of the Chao Phraya River, its original building now overshadowed by newer extensions which towered above it. But the original building was still very much in use. It contained the Oriental's most prestigious suites and it also contained the Author's Lounge, famous as the home of various literary figures who had spent time there in years gone by and who had while there penned some of the words of works that had become, and remained, famous ever since. These included Somerset Maugham and Noel Coward. The appearance of the lounge was very traditional and it was furnished with white wickerwork furniture topped with green cushions; it was a light and bright space. The most popular pastime for guests here was to take afternoon tea, a feast of scones, sandwiches and cakes served with exquisite delicacy by the silk clad waiters and waitresses who staffed the area. It was the opposite of cheap, but taking tea there provided a unique and memorable experience. Many permutations of refreshment were available and every patron seemed to regard it as special whatever they selected.

Alongside this lounge in the adjoining library was where *Khun* Katai held court. She undertook a key role in the hotel's incomparable customer services activity and had a desk at one end of the library where she was consulted about special requests and problems. Her job reflected the hotel's overall service philosophy, encapsulated in the saying: "Our job is to make the impossible possible." And by and large she did just that. This morning she had already supervised the photographing of the room used by one special regular and long stay guest. Such guests represented considerable income for the hotel and the photography was to make sure that if, or when, they returned, the staff on their floor could consult the photos and arrange their room just as the guest had favoured it on their last visit. She had also had to reassure a guest with a lizard phobia that, despite what he was convinced he had seen, there was definitely not one such resident in his room. Nothing less than evidence would do she felt, so she dispatched one of the reception staff to procure a lizard from the gardens, showed it to the guest in a paper bag with the brief comment "Gone now", and dispatched it back to the garden later.

Khun Katai had worked at the hotel for several decades since joining as a humble member of the housekeeping staff. Now, serene and professional looking in her colourful, silk suit, she had been presented with one of her favourite tasks. The booking she was considering, still a little way ahead, was for a short time - two nights. No matter: at The Oriental every individual guest was treated the same, they were important regardless of the length of their stay. This one she could sort without problem and create a special treat for the guests concerned. After a number of calls, internal and external, she had a list written below her original notes made from the first telephone call. Most things noted had a tick against them, others had a date alongside. All, she was sure, would be well.

✲

In their Phuket apartment overlooking the marina Poy had put down the telephone on *Khun* Katai confident that a suitable arrangement could be made. The hotel was world-renown and the lady she had spoken to exuded a quiet confidence and enthusiasm that made her think that any arrangement she made would be first class.

"Look at this" Michael said to Poy later in the afternoon when they had received an emailed note from *Khun* Katai listing her suggestions and arrangements. Poy leant over his shoulder as he sat at the computer and read it through.

"Okay, will do well, yes, will do very well."

He clicked on Forward, added a short note and sent it on its way to Philip.

"Okay, now we talk about visit to England" she followed up before he could become involved in anything else.

"Yes, right, I've printed out Philip's email about dates" he said, showing her a sheet of paper "and everything can be done, it seems to fit in pretty well with bookings here for trips. It avoids long made ones, and anyway most come to us at pretty short notice. If we are not here we are not here."

Poy resisted saying she had known it would be no problem, and pulled out their calendar and having studied Philip's note, grabbed a pencil and ruled a line through a three week period, she looked at Michael who nodded: "Okay," he said simply. It was done; his original thought of a mere two week trip disappeared as if in a puff of smoke. She opened a drawer in the desk and went over the line with a pen she took out. A red pen; change was now not an option.

"Okay, done" she said. "Now what we need, hotel, flight, more?"

"No need for a hotel," said Michael. "We can stay in Mum's house. Philip said we should ideally arrive on a Sunday so that he's able to collect us from the airport – Heathrow – it's a bit of a drive from Maldon, the traffic will be lighter on a Sunday and Philip can collect us as he won't be working. We've both kept our passports up over the years so that's no problem, but we need to check whether you need a visa, I think. Then we just book flights."

"No problem, I check for visa, you fix flights." Poy looked satisfied; they were going to England. Both of them. For three weeks too; she smiled. Job done. Almost.

"Now, when your house is sold will you buy house here or new boat?" They had talked a little about the money before. Given house values in England it would be a significant windfall but no conclusion had been reached, indeed Philip, out of touch with property values in the United Kingdom, had no accurate idea of what his mother's house might be worth. He didn't know enough about values but he did know that there would almost certainly be tax to pay, but at the mention of the sale like this Michael found himself in a something of a quandary. "Footloose" was without question of a certain age, a new – or newer - boat would be good, but he believed that the current boat's age and traditional style was part of its charm, he believed it was why many people decided to charter her. She was ... well, she was "Footloose"; there was no way he could get his head round the idea of her being replaced, after all

48

she had changed his life. This was the boat that had prompted him to stay in Thailand, setting up and running his business and which had introduced him to Poy too. He pondered for a moment, then spoke.

"Maybe we need a second boat" he said setting up the next point. "Then I would need an assistant."

"You *have* assistant" Poy said grinning, this had been a running joke ever since they had got together, "you have better than assistant. Have partner." And she punched his arm again.

"I am getting quite a bruise there" said Michael. "You're right, I know, but maybe this is an opportunity to expand the business."

They both smiled and agreed it needed more thought, meantime there were arrangements to be made. He needed to confirm dates with Philip before they made firm bookings about travel. Michael had never lived in his mother's house, nor even seen it, she had moved from the larger family home he remembered after his father had died and after Michael lost contact with them both and was in Thailand. Now this trip was definitely on he found that he was looking forward to it. He wondered what it would be like to be back in England and what memories it might reawaken for him; with that thought in mind, he went on line to check out flights.

CHAPTER FOUR

Surely it had moved

As they finished breakfast, their respective work schedules allowing them to do so together today, Philip and Miriam chatted about the forthcoming visit of Mac and Poy, an event now scheduled firm. Mac had booked the flights and emailed them their itinerary. Both of them looked forward to it, not only as a meeting of friends and as instrumental in completing matters relating to Abigail's estate and house, but also because their first meeting with Mac and Poy had been a part of their getting together when they visited Thailand. Having said he would help, Philip was already getting things organised for the visit.

"I have to meet the estate agent at Abigail's house at about six today after work. I'll be back as soon after that as I can."

The house in question was just along their road. In a street of terraced houses it was in fact very like his own though, as is common with terraced houses, they were mirror images. Abigail's affairs had been in limbo initially after her death, with it appearing at first that she had no relatives. But when Philip and Miriam had located her long-lost son, Philip had agreed with him that he would help with settling Abigail's affairs and getting the house ready for sale. They had seen the business Michael ran in Phuket, taking tourists for trips, and sailing lessons too, on his yacht "Footloose". Sailing was his life and he had made it clear that – money or no money - he had no desire to give that up and return to England, besides he ran the business with his Thai partner, Poy, and was very happy living in Thailand. When they had planned a visit however, and more recently set firm dates for it, Philip wanted to do all that he had promised to do ready for when they arrived. Getting started on the house, which was without doubt destined to be sold, was a major part of that.

Breakfast finished, Philip gave Miriam a hug, grabbed his bag from a chair in the hall and opened the front door to start his accustomed walk along the High Street to work. The small town still had a pretty traditional main street. There were not too many chains, though perhaps a surplus of cafes, and a number of traditional and useful retailers; Philip bemoaned the fact that the town had no bookshop. He saw a branch of W H Smith as no substitute, though there was a small antiquarian bookshop at the lower end of the street, which was a useful, but specialist, asset. The scale of it was such that the High Street was something of a community, especially amongst the smaller and independent shops, and Philip found himself greeting several people he knew as they began the process of opening up their shops.

✲

A little earlier and not far away as Terry Walsh had got up and made himself ready for school the house lights went out. No warning, just a click and his mobile phone, charging alongside him on the kitchen counter, beeped. He swore under his breath, but it was not dark outside and with the priorities of his age he was more concerned about his phone than the lights. In any case there was no question that the power was off. He knew his mother had been having problems with bills since she lost her job and she was always telling him "we can't afford it" in response to a variety of requests he made. He did check one or two other switches but, when nothing worked, it only took a moment for him to assume that the problem was that the bill was unpaid and the company had stopped the supply; for a moment also he wondered what to do, but time was pressing, he had been late getting up, and so he just grabbed his bag and set off for his walk to school. It was a problem, but a problem that would have to be addressed later.

"What do you think, Terry?" He had been miles away, but now was aware in a moment of the teacher talking to him from the front of the classroom. He looked blank and remained silent. He had been miles away, whatever the teacher had just said had passed him by. His silence confirmed the teacher's view.

"You have no idea what I just asked, have you?" the teacher persisted, adding that Terry should stay behind and see him at the end of the class as Terry continued to remain silent, conscious of his classmates looking at him.

"You have to learn to concentrate, Terry."

As his fellow pupils streamed out of the room at the end of the lesson, Terry stood by the teacher's desk apprehensive and wondering what punishment might be imminent. "You're usually a bright one about questions, always ready to have your say."

"Yes, Sir, sorry," Terry sounded contrite.

"Is everything alright at home?" The teacher asked, taking him onto territory he would much rather not talk about. The pause was tiny, then the words came out automatically.

"Yes, Sir."

"Well let's have no more of this daydreaming in future, I'll be watching you. Off you go."

The teacher's view of his past record saved him, Terry mumbled something indistinct and headed for the door suitably chastened. He knew the teacher was right and he did not like having his inattention pointed out to him; he was doing okay at school and took some pride in his performance. For a tiny instant the thought had come into his mind of saying that, no, things were very much not all right at home, of confessing his situation and demanding help. But this lasted little more than an instant. He was upset, he missed his Mum for all her faults; but he would not allow himself to think anything other than that she must be coming back soon. In all honesty he was finding things difficult, but he was also fearful. What if she was not coming back, what then? He knew the answer. There was no way someone would come and switch the lights back on and allow him to continue to live in his own home alone. He would be taken into care. Into care: those two short words had a terrifying feel to them. He knew someone at school whose parents had been going through a messy divorce, the father was hounding the mother and she couldn't cope with three children. The boy Terry knew had disappeared, rehoused too far away to continue at the same school. Terry had heard no more about it, but he was pretty sure it wasn't good. The words invited the prospect not just of something unknown but of something unpleasant: people he didn't know, rules he didn't like, and maybe too a place far away from those he knew; perhaps far enough away to necessitate his attending a different school. So he had said "Yes, Sir" to the teacher's question, and now the moment with the teacher had passed and he had said nothing about the real situation.

In fact he had told one person his secret. He had told his friend Jackson about it all, the No-Mum situation as he called it. He had sworn him to secrecy and Jackson had agreed to say nothing, but more and more he told Terry that he had to tell someone.

It had come up earlier in the morning as they had gone to their first class together and Terry had added the vanishing electricity to his catalogue of misfortunes.

"How long can you go on like this?" Jackson had said. "And now with no electric, what about charging your phone? It's not right, but no, before you ask, I won't say anything. I promised, didn't I? No sweat. But just do it. Tell *someone.* You can't just ignore it all." Hearing about the electricity Jackson's first thought too had been about the phone. And the computer: he and Jackson had decided to work together on the special school project – "the project" as they called it – and without their computers no progress could be made.

"You'll need to sort the electrics or the project will be held up" said Jackson. "It's not just your phone you won't be able to charge. There can't be any heat. You must tell someone."

But Terry was still hesitant and besides, even if he did tell someone, he couldn't decide who to tell and, for the moment he felt he couldn't draw attention to himself; the prospect of being taken into care was all pervading. Besides, first things first, he had had an idea that would at least ease the electricity problem. Meantime he was glad he had told Jackson, his best friend, about his situation. He was not only a good friend, one Terry judged would keep a secret if asked, he was also adopted. Somehow there seemed to be a link there with the situation he feared most.

After having words with the teacher Terry found that Jackson had waited for him outside the classroom door and they went off to lunch together. He and Jackson had been friends throughout their time at school and they had become closer still in the last year or two. This was in part because Jackson's father had bought a boat. This at once reinforced Terry's vision of a family much better off than his own, but Maldon was on the estuary of the River Blackwater, there were hundreds of boats moored at a number of sailing clubs ranged along both shores of the wide estuary that the narrow river became after flowing through the town. In fact the boat wasn't new and did not represent a huge investment. The wide reaches of the Blackwater estuary was a great place to sail. When Jackson went out on the boat with his father, it was an eighteen foot sailing boat with a small two berth cabin, he liked to have someone his own age with him and Terry had spent a good deal of time sailing with them. The estuary was an interesting place to sail: they could go round Northey Island, or Osea, another island, both of them connected to the shore by causeways uncovered at low tide and the building of which dated from Roman times. They could go further afield, to Bradwell where the old nuclear power station was provisionally scheduled to be replaced by a new one to be built by the Chinese; not something that was popular with many local people concerned about the effect on the environment. Many felt that a nuclear facility on the shore was a nonsense in an age of global warming and rising sea levels. Or they could go further down the estuary to Mersey Island where the estuary broadened further and met the sea. Terry found it all great fun. In fact he was hooked; his only complaint was that, as the visitor as it were, he could not spend as much time at the helm as he would have liked to do. He dreamed of a boat of his own, but he knew it was not about to be a realistic prospect. Fat chance, he thought, especially at present.

You're a natural Terry" Jackson's dad had told him on one occasion after he'd done a stint at the helm. He did not know about that, but he just knew he felt very comfortable in a boat and sometimes wondered if there was any way that sailing could be part of his future. In fact, like most kids his age, he spent little time thinking far ahead; more often than not he felt that Friday week seemed like a long way off.

There was something Terry wanted to investigate with his friend.

"Can I ask you a question?" Terry swallowed a mouthful of lunch before speaking.

"Course" said Jackson his voice indistinct projected through a mouthful of food.

"What's it like being adopted then J?" he asked. He always called Jackson J, since saying to him once way back "What sort of name is Jackson?" Jackson had taken no offense, agreeing it was unusual and more often acted as a surname and they had agreed on his using J in future. Just between friends.

"It's no big deal," said Jackson. "I was adopted as a baby, once I was older I think I've always known, it was never a secret, and anyway Mum and Dad are okay, they've never treated me any different because of it."

"Right." Terry dropped his enquiry, and mentioned the boat.

"It's a pity *Seascape* has to be ashore at this time of year, isn't it?"

"Suppose, but most everyone brings them ashore through the winter. I know Dad said something about the insurance covering nothing outside the sailing season, if you had your boat damaged in a winter storm you'd get nothing. Besides think of that cold water." He gave an exaggerated shiver.

"I hope I can come with you sometimes when sailing starts again," said Terry "I really enjoy it."

"I'd never have guessed!" Jackson thought back to their times on the river and grinned as he said it, continuing: "Course you can. Dad's said we can take her out on our own sometimes next season. He said we are old enough and don't act like duffers. Why duffers?" Terry knew that.

"It's from *Swallows and Amazons,* remember. Come on, we got to be back in class, I've already got one telling off today, for day dreaming."

They hurried together towards their next class, but much of Terry's mind was elsewhere; while he was no closer to telling anyone, and still wondered who would be right, he was working on the germ of an idea, something that he felt might help his situation; at least a bit.

CHAPTER FIVE

It was only temporary

With no electricity in the house, Terry was at the point where he had had to reconsider his situation. He was of an age now where day to day he did not see all that much of his mother, he sort of took her for granted and accepted her as she was without very much thought. He went off to school early and she was sometimes still in bed. When he came home, almost every day she would have supper ready for him, but if he was honest they did not talk much in the evening when he had homework, friends to see and a computer in his bedroom on which he spent more time than he should. In the summer though he was out more, most often with Jackson and, whenever possible, out on the boat. Then everything had changed: he had come in one evening and she wasn't there. No note, no supper… and no sign of her since. She was depressed he knew, his father had left them when he was small and Terry knew she had always struggled to bring him up alone; since she lost her job though everything had got worse. He realised that if his mother did not return home soon then he was in big trouble: no light, no power and, with mounting horror he also realised what a long list of things this ruled out: no charging his phone or anything else and no television. Or heating, as Jackson had pointed out. For the moment, he could do nothing, he was in danger of being late for school and he finished up breakfast and left the house in a rush. He brooded about the problem all day, wondering what to do, and unaware of the sequence of letters lying unopened and out of sight in a kitchen drawer chasing payment and forewarning of the electricity supply being cut off if the amount due was not paid at once. Apart from anything else he worried about "the project"; he had to be able to work on his computer. But he did have one idea about his situation, one that had come to mind the previous day; though he had thought more about it, he had done nothing about it during the previous evening. He had been busy with homework after a rudimentary supper by the light of candles he had found in a kitchen cupboard. One more day on, he now felt it was worth pursuing.

Once home after school he changed out of his school clothes and went out and walked a little way along the road to his Aunt Abigail's house. She was not his real aunt, but he called her that and she was always friendly to him when she saw him, even though his mother had not kept in close contact with her since his father left. His father had worked as a jobbing gardener and was employed part time by Abigail's husband before he died and she had moved to the smaller house just along the road. He knew she had died a while ago, his mother had been bad around that time, many a day she had not come out of her bedroom; he remembered that she had not gone to the funeral, though there had been a brief note about it in the local paper. He also knew that Abigail's house had since stood empty, someone on the street had told him that the house was to be sold, but that depended on her son returning. It seemed he was working somewhere overseas. Terry knew nothing of him; his disappearance had been long before Terry was born.

He glanced around him. The street was quiet, no one was nearby. He went through the front gate, shutting it behind him and being careful not to let it bang. Then he went round to the back of the house. It was all shut up. Of course it was, why would he think otherwise? He examined all the windows at the back and checked the back door itself: all were locked tight. The kitchen was an extension standing out from the house with a flat roof and above that was the window of the bathroom. That frosted glass window looked the least secure. He stood on the wheeled rubbish bin, which he pulled into the corner where the kitchen jutted out from the line of the main house and from there he climbed up the drainpipe and scrambled over the guttering onto the flat roof. It was a stretch: he hung for a moment at the gutter, legs waving in the air behind him, before he scrabbled onto the roof. He stood upright, brushed small stones and moss off his sweatshirt, and looked around. Using a bit of loose tile he found lying on the flat roof he prised open the bathroom window; it took a while but he did not want to damage anything, he needed it to close again and be secure. Once it was open he climbed inside and into the bath, which was situated just below the window. No real damage had been done and he was able to close the window again behind him, making it secure or as secure as such an old window could be. He rinsed the bath out where he had left marks from his shoes. He then took his shoes off and went forward in his socks.

The house was quiet. He went down the stairs, illuminated only by the tiny light of a smoke alarm, pausing for a few moments half way down and standing silent and listening. For a minute it felt a bit eerie, the feeling of the house being empty was intimidating, even though he had persuaded himself beforehand that it would be a solution, at least to some of his problems. The moment passed and he continued to the bottom. The kitchen was neat and tidy in a way that could say nothing but 'unoccupied'. He found the key was in the back door; that was good. He could get in and out. He told himself Aunt Abigail wouldn't mind, it was just until his Mum got back after all. He clicked the kitchen light on, and found to his satisfaction that he now had somewhere to be with electricity. He closed the living room curtains at the front of the house, and slipped out of the front door for a moment to check that no light showed to passers-by on the street. It didn't, well very little, and anyway over recent weeks he had noticed as he had gone by that a light showed there at night as if on a timer. It seemed unlikely anyone would notice his presence. Having looked in the kitchen cupboards and found a packet of biscuits, put the kettle on and made himself tea, he found that of course he had no milk. A little nonplussed he looked round and spotted an envelope on the kitchen table marked "Milkman". It was unsealed and he could see a ten pound note sticking out of it. In fact, with coins too, there was almost twenty pound in it. Rationalising that what he was doing "was temporary, just until Mum returns and that Aunt Abigail wouldn't mind" he went out and bought a few supplies, including some milk, cereal and bread.

Back in the house he found various things in the kitchen cupboards and had sardines on toast for supper in front of the television while his phone glowed, a tiny red spot indicating it was charging in the corner of the room. The heating seemed to have been set to keep the chill off the place and the time that followed proved to be the best evening he had had for a while. Later, after a quick look round to make sure everything was neat and lights switched off, he put his shoes back on and left by the back door, locking it after himself and taking the key with him. He had no wish to leave the house open to any lowlife that might be around, indeed he had convinced himself that his visit — or visits, because he very much intended to return - would do no harm. And next time he would not have to climb in via the roof.

Over the following few days he came and went to the house a number of times. He ate supper there, charged his phone and laptop, watched Abigail's television and, with his laptop powered up, he did his homework and also worked a bit on "the project". He always left the place pretty much as he had found it, but did not duplicate the precise state it had been in when he had first gone in. It didn't occur to him that doing so was of any consequence.

But, of course, he wasn't the sole visitor the house was receiving at present.

✶

Philip had been in Abigail's house for half an hour or so and, whiling away the minutes until the estate agent came, and he had found something strange. It followed an odd experience in the library too, one which like Terry's problem, involved electricity. He was to be last away at the end of the day and, as he locked up, without any warning he found himself plunged into darkness. Well, not total darkness, there was still some light outside, but the inside of the library was very gloomy; the ranks of shelving cast random, gloomy shadows across the main public space. As he headed for the back door alongside which was located the fuse box, he thought he heard movement, a sound that seemed to him very like footsteps. Was there someone still in the building? Once the thought was in his mind he became a little paranoid. There was no clear view across the main library floor, of course: it was blocked by ranks of shelves. Feeling he had to check, he retraced his steps and did a complete circuit of the area. He found no one, though he felt it would not be very difficult for an intruder to keep some shelving between them and remain hidden. It went to the back door again, opened the fuse box and saw at once that something had tripped the power. He threw the switch. The lights came on. Something had acted to trip it out, maybe he thought, remembering a job put off too long, the battered old kettle in the back office. It was due for renewal and he made a note in his office about it. Equally it could just have been a twitch in the supply, something that happened from time to time locally, especially in the winter months. He had one more look round before he left and, as he did so, he noticed something else: there was another of what Miriam had called the "countdown cards", a third one, pinned on the notice board. He could have sworn it wasn't there just half an hour ago, when he had been that way. Its form was the same, a yellow postcard with the date and a typed message, this one said: DON'T LET TIME CATCH YOU OUT. It had the present day's date on it. The cards and their purpose was becoming more and more puzzling he thought, maybe he had heard someone while the lights were out, but he was pretty sure that there was no one there now. Spooky. He remembered his appointment, put the card in his desk drawer, left and locked the main door and hastened down the High Street.

The estate agent was late for their appointment, well not late exactly, she had agreed to meet him after the library closed and said she would be there between 7.15 and 7.30; now the first was perhaps proving a bit early for her. He had already done a small amount of clearing up around the house and a black plastic sack sat in the hall with a little rubbish in it. He stopped puzzling about the mysterious "countdown cards" in the library, which had been on his mind walking from work, though he still had no theory about them, and turned his mind to the clear up looking for something useful to fill just a few minutes before the agent arrived. On the kitchen wall was a pin board, a fabric board crossed with strips to hold paper items tucked underneath. Standing in the kitchen, realising he could not make a cup of tea as there would be no milk, he thought he would clear it. One small job done. There were handwritten notes, now long out of date, shopping lists and reminders of various sorts, and also a profusion of business cards. Some had no doubt been put through the letterbox by people touting for business. They were those of emergency plumbers, electricians, a number of restaurants - some cards, some menus — even one from an estate agent suggesting a valuation be made as properties were in high demand in the area. Philip wondered how long that had been posted there; it was not from the agent due to visit this evening.

He began to take them down, feeling that there was no merit in their staying up now the house was empty and the kitchen would look neater without them once prospective buyers began to be shown round the house in due course. He gathered a handful, took a few steps into the hall and put them in the rubbish bag. Gathering more, one at the bottom of a small stack caught his eye. It was the business card of a private detective. That struck him as odd, as far as he was aware it wasn't a category of business that canvassed for business with door to door circulars as a rule and he couldn't imagine that Abigail had used such a service. He was turning it over in his hand when he was startled as the doorbell rang. It must be the estate agent. He shoved the card in his pocket, dumped the others he'd collected with it in the rubbish bag as he went through the hall and opened the front door.

"Thank you for coming" he said as he shook hands with a young woman who was smartly dressed and who was, in his estimation, in her late twenties, though she still struck Philip as somewhat young for the role. She carried a briefcase from which she took a clipboard and a large measuring tape. They introduced themselves.

"It's a very nice house" she said "and this is a good address, a quiet street yet so convenient for the town. I think you'll find it fetches a good price. May I ask what you paid for it?"

"Oh, it's not my house," replied Philip, thinking that it was pretty much the mirror image of his own place a few doors along the road of terraced properties and pleased to hear that the value was good. "It belonged to a friend, a lady who died a little while back, her son lives and works overseas and I'm getting things organised for when he visits. Then it can go on the market. Can you work out a value and draw up the details you would put out about it so that I can have that ready to show him?"

"Yes, of course" she smiled. "May I know who ..." She paused.

"Oh, yes, of course, the name's Michael, Michael Croft."

"Right," she made a note. "Do you know when he'll be here?"

"Yes, it's all planned, not far ahead now. I'll let you have the exact dates when you've let me have your details. Meantime, continue to liaise with me, okay?" he had given his details when they spoke on the telephone to make the arrangement to meet.

She nodded. He followed her round as she measured and wrote notes, also asking him a few questions as they went like how old the boiler was, to which he did not know the answers. And some to which he did, like the Council tax band; which he assumed was the same as his own property. She took some photographs.

Back in the kitchen she asked "Okay, what about the garden?"

"Right." Philip hadn't thought about that. He went to the back door.

"That's odd, I thought there was a key in the back door, but never mind, we can get round the side. Follow me."

They exited out the front door, walked round to the back through a narrow passage and the agent made a brief note adding the garden details to the spec then returning to get back in the warm. Then, promising to get back to him soon having written a description of the property and with a recommended selling price, she pronounced it a "highly saleable property", took her leave and disappeared up the road towards the High Street where her office was located. Philip went back into the house to ensure he was leaving everything all straight. He wanted the place to be tidy when Mac and Poy arrived from Thailand. He stood for a moment in the kitchen. He had been in and out of the house a number of times in recent days, in part to check all was well, and also to get ready for the viewing visits that the place would see once it was cleared and ready for sale to tie in with Mac's visit. He had made tea a few times, but he was sure he had put everything away. After all, when he visited Abigail before she died he had almost always been the one to make the tea; he knew where things went.

Now however, he noticed to his surprise that there was a mug turned upside down on the plate rack alongside the sink. Surely he had not left it like that, he thought. As he looked it seemed to him that the sugar jar had perhaps moved too. He did not take sugar so he would not have done that. For a few seconds, perhaps with thoughts of Mary Donaldson's talk of contacting the dead lurking in his brain, he found himself wondering if Abigail was still around in some way, giving the kitchen a little tidy and preparing for his next visit.

He shivered; for a second he had that "someone's walked over my grave feeling" and felt that maybe Abigail's presence did linger in the house in some way. But he knew that couldn't be. He dismissed the thought as soon as it formed viewing it as just the classic, though ill-defined, feeling empty houses can sometimes give you, and with the business card he had found and kept for the moment forgotten in his pocket, Philip exited the front door and walked at a brisk pace on towards his own home, but he found himself wondering again as he did so about the mug: surely, he thought, it had moved.

CHAPTER SIX

Maybe someone else was the answer

Philip didn't know what to do. He was not a great worrier, though at present the question of wedding arrangements was on his mind. In a constructive way he liked to think. He did have one idea for the future he felt Miriam would like, but the wedding was another matter, one that still needed some working out and he guessed Miriam would begin to press him about it before too long. Meantime he was thinking of Mary Donaldson; she was a regular visitor to the library and he knew he was almost bound to see her today. He had promised to speak to her again, but he really wasn't sure what he could say. He had broached the subject with Miriam at breakfast time.

"Do you remember Mary Donaldson?" he had said.

"You mean my paint sprayer?" she replied, spreading marmalade on her toast with a precision that Philip found impressive to see so early in the day.

"Yes, well I sort of promised her I would speak to her again about things and today's the day she always comes into the library."

"And you want me to do what? You know she can make a complaint, but, as I told you, it's such a difficult area, I can't see her getting any satisfaction. It might just upset her more, you know. It's perhaps better to encourage her to forget all about it." Her comment left Philip nonplussed, but he pursued it a little more.

"Surely there is more that could be done than that. That woman is a fraud, she preys on vulnerable people."

"I know. I agree. But that doesn't stop it from being difficult." Philip looked at her hard.

"Difficult how exactly?" he asked. Miriam swallowed the last of her toast, took a swig of her coffee and looked pointedly at the clock on the kitchen wall.

"I must go" she said, standing up and clearing her breakfast things away, "but essentially it's because it's bound up with vague concepts. Intent, for instance, does the person intend to defraud, ˑd is the payment made willingly; some people get comfort from ˑt of thing, you know. Belief is involved too: does the person ˑ they *are* in touch with the dead?"

ˑ, it's obvious this woman doesn't think that. ˑe's no such thing as ghosts." A thought

70

flashed through Philip's mind: unless Abigail is haunting the kitchen in her old house, or some admin-happy ghost is posting notices in the library, in which case he might have to change his mind. He didn't mention either possibility, and Miriam continued.

"I agree. But I certainly don't have time to debate that now. Duty calls. Trust me it is difficult, but I promise we will talk about it some more. Maybe…" A thought flashed across her mind, but she continued: "I will think about it. Forget it for the moment, anyway you've a wedding to plan, remember."

Miriam's face seemed to indicate they were at a dead end. Only for the moment thought Philip as he became all the more resolved to do… well, to do something. Nevertheless they parted company agreeing to leave it for the moment and went off towards their respective day's work.

The library was not too busy. Though quite soon after arriving he had heard two bizarre questions: "Do you have that horse book? The one with the blue cover." Even if the often made presumption that a book with an unremembered title could be identified just by the colour of its cover was correct, he had found that people's conviction about the colour of book covers was not a hundred percent accurate either; in fact it was more often than not plain wrong. So it was with this book, some moments of prompting identified it as "War Horse" and the cover was not blue. And the second question, asked by a man rushing and in a hurry: "Do you have a book about caring for pet guinea pigs?" This too had led to a small exchange, with Philip checking and explaining that they did have one, though it was out on loan at present but due back soon. This was followed by the enquirer saying: "Never mind, I'll have to buy something quick otherwise the little buggers will starve. Kids, eh!" The man returned to rush mode, turned on his heel and left. Philip could have offered to reserve the book, but it seemed that would be too late to avoid the starvation of his children's pets.

Later on when Mary Donaldson came in as expected she spotted him at the front desk and came straight over.

"Hello, Mr Marchington," she began. "Did you find out anything for me?" A momentary concern showed in her face and she added "Oh, you do remember my problem don't you, it was so kind of you to offer to help."

"Of course I do, and please it's Philip; remember you asked me to call you Mary?"

"Yes, yes, of course."

"I have to say Mary, that at present I've not got very far. It is difficult. I've done some checking and it's a question of proof, I'm told – your word against..."

"That awful woman," Mary pitched in. "Well, thanks for trying, it's such a shame though. I just don't want someone else to be fleeced. I had hoped there was something that could be done." Philip saw her face register disappointment, then resignation. He could almost feel her resolving to forget all about it as he continued:

"Hang on, don't despair, I have not given up yet, in fact I think there may be something to be done. I'm still investigating, just leave it with me a while longer and check again with me next time you're in."

Mary thanked him left a book with him and went to choose a new one. Philip stood silent for a moment, recalling what she had said and her all too apparent upset; he hoped he was not being overconfident, but maybe the answer lay with someone else's speaking to the dead.

✻

A few days later Philip drove in to the library in the morning. This was not his usual practice; unless the weather was terrible he enjoyed his walk to work. But today he needed the car. Now it was his lunch break. He had made the appointment for the middle of the day, in part to minimise the importance in his own mind of what he was doing, it's just a brief interlude in the day he told himself, but he didn't believe it. Nor in fact did he believe that he could keep what he was about to do secret from Miriam, though that had, if he was honest with himself, been another reason for sandwiching it into the middle of a working day when they would not meet up until the evening.

The matter of Mary Donaldson had assumed growing importance to him and he had felt there must be something else he could do. So now he was in an area of Maldon away from the town centre, so he could park hassle free at the roadside with no penalty. He did so, walking the final few yards along what was a nice residential street, one with houses set back some distance from the road, till he saw the right number. Neatly cut grass ran down to the pavement across an open unfenced frontage and looking at the sizable house prompted the thought that they must be worth some money. He walked up the path and rang the doorbell. No sound from inside the house was audible outside, but after a moment the door was soon opened and Jane Wearing stood in front of him. She was dressed in a low key tweedy suit, pearls at her neck, and apart from what struck Philip as a rather odd hairstyle, she was not the least extraordinary.

"Hello, you must be James Tomlinson, please, do come in."

She spoke pleasantly, reminding him by the way she addressed him that he had used a false name when he made the appointment to see her. Jim Tomlinson was a saxophonist and the husband of his musical favourite, jazz singer Stacey Kent.

"Yes. Okay, thanks" said Philip, hoping that he was not sounding as nervous as he now found himself feeling. In her line of work Jane Wearing must be used to nervous clients, but his particular reason for feeling nervous was, he presumed, different from most. She led the way through the hall to a room, which he imagined was a dining room in the original configuration of the house, but now set up for her consultations. A round table was set in the middle of the room, covered by a dark green cloth that almost reached the floor around it. Two red candles were lit and stood in a stainless steel candlestick on a sideboard alongside and, at the rear of the room, French windows gave access onto a small, tidy garden. A long drape of dark material hung along one wall of the room. He could just hear the sound of the birds singing outside, although the doors were closed.

There were two chairs. A carafe of water and several glasses were set out on her side of the table on a silver salver. Jane asked if he wanted a drink.

"Does that offer include tea?" Philip felt he could do with a drink, having worked through to the time he left the library.

"Well …" there was the slightest sound in Jane's voice that suggested that she had not meant tea, but just a glass of water. Nevertheless she seemed to be at some pains to create a happy client and went on "…of course, just give me moment."

She left the room for the kitchen, which seemed to be next door. He heard a kettle click on and there was the sound of china being moved about. The pause gave Philip a moment to think, he looked around the room. It was, well, it was ordinary was the only word that came to mind. Bland too. There were no pictures, a couple of simple ornaments on the sideboard were all that softened the appearance, one a cut glass fruit bowl, and there was a total lack of what he imagined to be the classic tools of the trade as it were: no crystal ball; no skulls; no sign of the occult. Nothing untoward, nothing to even give a clue as to the sort of things that took place here. Philip smiled to himself, this was getting silly, and he knew that there would be nothing like that. But he remained intent on checking her out, his thought being that personal experience of her sessions might give him an idea of what to do next; if anything else could be done.

She came back into the room and put down a cup of tea on a small tray that also contained milk and sugar. Philip thanked her and added some milk. She drew the thick curtains leaving the room lit by the candles alone and sat down.

"How can I help you?" she asked. "I take it from what you said on the telephone that you've lost someone." She had quizzed him on the phone a little and he had told her it was about a death.

"Yes, my sister." Philip's sister was alive and well living down in Kent, he had spoken to her just the other day involving her in his tentative and still unresolved wedding planning, but he had no intention of talking about a real lost relative, especially not his late wife, even though time had passed and he now had Miriam in his life, her death would always be emotional to recall.

"Tell me about her."

Philip told her a little, he based the facts on his sister, but found he used dates and certain details from his wife's situation, just, he told himself, so that he told a consistent story – he couldn't have his sister dying on two different dates because he could not remember something he had invented. Jane probed further and Philip tried to say as little as possible, he was aware of the way such people are said to read their clients, picking up clues from everything they say. And from their manner too it seemed; Philip hoped his manner, and he found he was somewhat nervous about his plan, was not inadvertently creating suspicion. Even so he found it was a little difficult to play the part he had invented for himself. The information he did provide mounted up despite his trying to waffle and not give away too many useful facts.

Half an hour or so went by, during which Jane either asked questions, made sympathetic comments about his doubtless grief, saying it was to be expected, and how "time was a great healer". His mind wandered, in his experience time changed nothing, the only thing that had changed things for him since his wife had died had been prompted by action; and, if he was honest, by some good fortune along the way. Jane continued speaking, mainly reiterating information Philip had given her in a rather different form or sequence. Then she changed tack. She closed her eyes and sat still and silent; Philip found the silence awkward, but realised it was doubtless all part of the patter, if patter could include silence.

"I am getting a very clear picture of her now" she said "not physically, I don't see the colour of her eyes or anything, but I do feel her presence. Be still please."

There followed several minutes of silence, during which Jane sat with closed eyes and Philip gave the green check pattern on the tablecloth close inspection and wondered about the eyes comment. The woman was more likely to be taking time to compose a shopping list, he thought, than getting in touch with the departed. If she was truly psychic then he imagined that she would know that his sister was alive and well. Then she interrupted his thoughts and spoke again.

"She wants to speak to you. She's been trying to get through to you, but it's difficult… it seems she may have nearly made contact. Have you had a telephone call recently, when there appeared to no one there when you answered?"

Philip found what he had just been asked incredible. Given the prevalence of calls from the likes of those selling solar panels or intent on checking whether you had been inappropriately sold PPI or had an accident and the use of automatic dialling systems, was there *anyone* who had not received such a call? It seemed impossible that such a ploy would persuade anyone but the terminally gullible of a ghostly contact in a million years. But he presumed she said it because it worked on many of her clients. He realised the pause he was introducing was getting longer and, aiming to keep up the pretence, he continued, speaking up again, putting a little hesitation

77

into his voice and trying, despite his sense of the ridiculous, to sound sober.

"Well, perhaps, there was one occasion..." He let his voice tail off. He was thankful Jane did not refer directly to his answer, he would not have known what on earth to say next.

"She certainly has a message for you" she continued "there are things she wants you to know, but I am afraid she's slipped away now. We were so close, so very close." She smiled at him. No doubt it was intended to be reassuring, but it reminded Philip of some mothers he saw in the library giving their children a smile that said "Enough." She continued.

"I'm sure she's happy. I am also sure we will be able to make contact next time. Yes, quite sure. I know she wants it. She does. She knows you need it. She knows you need to move on. She will speak to you soon."

Nothing had been said about the second appointment that was doubtless being implied by what she had said, though Philip had no morsel of an intention of booking one. She was also apparently signalling that they were at the end of their session. He resisted the strong temptation to launch into a rant, though he was now even more certain that she was a fraud than he had been when he had first spoken to Mary Donaldson and heard about her experience; he could not imagine anything changing his mind. His mind raced for a moment as he tried to collect his thoughts.

"I have left my diary on my desk" he said, "but I'll give you a call about coming again, if I may. Meantime, what do I owe you now?"

She had made it clear on the telephone that fifty pounds was the fee, and she repeated that now. Philip reached into his jacket and laid an envelope containing the appropriate amount of cash he had prepared before leaving the library on the table; a cheque would have given away his name. She did not reach for it, perhaps, he thought, not wanting to emphasise the financial nature of their meeting. Their business was concluded for the moment but for one thing Philip wanted to bring up. It was clear that she pretended to summon messages from the dead, but Philip wanted to check on what else she might claim. The more he found out about her the more certain he felt that he would be able to think of something he could do for Mary.

"Before I go," he said as he rose, "there's another thing I wanted to ask: do you think your gift could help locate someone who's gone missing? It's not suspicious or anything, just two people who have lost touch and where one wants to find the other." He hoped he had said the word gift without the sarcasm he felt being apparent.

"Is this recent?"

"Yes", said Philip, wondering as he did so why he had elected to say that.

"Then next time, I may well be able to help" she said, "especially if you bring something belonging to the missing person – a procession can often help establish a link." Philip lodged another doubtless false claim to her list of crimes. She continued:

"But locating a person who has gone missing may be straightforward, and I've a friend who tackles this kind of thing. He's very good and the sooner you start, the clearer the trail may be." She crossed to the sideboard, reached into a drawer and returned to give him a business card: it said "Gary Hunt. Private Detective. Confidentiality assured". Philip made no comment about that and thanked her, the thanks sticking in his throat. He stood up and moved towards the hall with Jane Wearing following.

"See you again soon," she replied "and one more thing. I have a feeling. I think you will receive a small surprise on your journey to work, quite soon, I believe." Philip almost responded by saying something about his regular walk to work but he stopped himself, though he did wonder why she had thrown in this additional comment. He liked being able to walk to work in a manageable time, but it had to be said that doing so was almost always totally uneventful; well with the notable exception of when he had found Abigail's body. Back in the hall, she held the front door open for him, they exchanged goodbyes and Philip retreated down the path and walked along the road.

Back in the car, Philip sat looking again at the card she had given him and gave it closer inspection. It was a more recent printing, more modern and was in colour, doubtless ordered from the internet. But he was pretty sure that it was the same name and address as on the card he had found in Abigail's house. He remembered putting that card in his jacket pocket. He felt for it and found it was still there and, on examination, it was soon apparent that it was the same man. A private detective called Hunt: the thought of such a name amused him. But the coincidence puzzled him. He started the car and hurried back to the library, even though he had extended it, his allotted lunch break would soon be over. Now he was in charge he liked to set a good example about such things. He drove on feeling that the meeting had very much reinforced his opinion that the woman was a charlatan.

But he was soon to discover that she was a charlatan with friends.

He left the car is his reserved parking spot behind the library and later, as he walked home at the end of the day, he felt that he had achieved something, he had something to tell Miriam and it might be that it would help in finding something to do for Mary Donaldson. He crossed the road on the pedestrian crossing at the top of the High Street outside the church. Doing so always reminded him of how his first dinner with Miriam had been arranged when they had bumped into each other on this very spot. He walked on, turning left to go down the main run of the High Street. As he did so something seen out of the corner of his eye caught his attention. On the notice board outside the church amongst the posters and injunctions to attend local events was something familiar: a yellow postcard-sized card. It matched the form of the ones that had mysteriously appeared in the library, except that this time it was wrapped in plastic, no doubt to protect it from the elements, and the name Philip appeared at the top above another typed message reading: YOU REALLY MUSTN'T FORGET. He unpinned it, then looked round to see if anyone had noticed what he was doing and, seeing no one taking an interest, put it in his pocket, wondering as he did so if this qualified as Jane Wearing's small surprise even though it was on the way home from work rather than to it. It was a surprise, but seemed likely to be just a coincidence rather than providing proof of her predictive powers, he thought. But what were these cards all about? This, he thought, is getting silly; or spooky.

CHAPTER SEVEN

It was a good idea

Philip had arranged to meet Margaret, his youngest assistant, before the end of the day and she sat on the other side of his desk looking expectant and holding the notebook she always seemed to carry in her hand. He wished his office was larger, there was no room for a separate table, and meetings across the desk always seemed to be a little formal.

"I am doing a reading at one of the regular schools later in the week," he said, "I'd like you to come too."

"Right. Okay, but why?" she looked puzzled.

"Well it's currently something I do, when Froby was around then I was frankly happy to do as many as possible just to be out of her way for a while." They exchanged grins knowing that both of them had disliked the woman, and Philip wished he had actually said "out of her clutches" rather than opting for something essentially bland. "Now I'm in charge," he continued, "it's difficult to give the same time to them, yet I believe it's an important activity.

I need a deputy." He had always had an evangelical approach to the library, seeing it as a force for good, he had always been passionate about children and reading in particular, indeed some of the kids he first met on school reading sessions later visited the library and some of them became enthusiastic regulars.

"You want me to do the reading?" Margaret posed it as a question and looked appalled at the thought.

"Well, not immediately, the idea is that you should come to one with me, see how it goes, then we can talk about it some more. I'll make sure you are okay with it first. I think you'd find it fun and I'm sure you would do it very well."

Margaret looked relieved, well a little, and they talked about it some more until finally she seemed to be at least open to the idea. Philip resolved to work on it; she had the potential to do well he felt and this task would give her an extra activity and a responsibility specific to her. Matters were left like that for the moment; he would talk to her again after she had accompanied him.

A few moments after Margaret had left the office, she was back again. The door was open, as it usually was, and she stood in the doorway and pitched straight in.

"Me again" she said "someone's asking for you." Margaret stood looking into the cubby-hole Philip laughingly referred to as his office and where he sat at his desk surrounded by papers. After he had spoken with her about the school visit it was admin time.

"What's it about?" He responded, half hoping it was something more interesting than what he was now supposed to be engaged in for the next hour or two; it was not his favourite part of the job.

"It's the lady who cried, you know, Mary Donaldson, she says you'll know what it's about. I sat her down at the corner table and said I'd try to find you. What *is* it about?" Philip reckoned she was entitled to ask, she had, after all, been the one who had found Mary crying a few days ago.

"It's a long story. Tell me, do you believe in ghosts? No matter. I'll tell you about it later."

Margaret looked puzzled, as well she might in face of such a question; she didn't think she did believe in ghosts, despite her grandmother swearing she had seen one at nearby Beeleigh Abbey. The house, for long owned by members of the Foyle family, owners of Foyles famous bookshops, was more than old enough to be a candidate for such things. But that was years ago. Philip offered no more insight on the matter, just got up saying he would deal with it and hurried off to see Mary.

It was quiet at the far end of the library, though one elderly man was snoozing in front of an open magazine lying flat on the table. Though his head lolled forward Philip recognised him as a regular, he didn't know his name but sometimes wondered what stopped him sleeping at night, as he seemed to spend regular time dozing over a paper or magazine in the library. As Philip approached he could see Mary sitting alone at one of the other tables.

"Hello, Mary, this isn't your regular day." He smiled at her.

"No, I know, but I was in the High Street and I wondered..." Her voice tailed off.

"Well, I'm still not sure what can be done, I'm afraid, but I do understand your feelings a whole lot better now. I have been doing some research. I went to see Jane Wearing. Just yesterday in fact."

Mary's eyes widened with surprise "My goodness. What did you say to her? Did you mention me? I don't want to get in any trouble you know."

"No, I didn't mention you, and the paint is all gone now by the way, I'm sure that episode is best forgotten. I didn't go to lay into her either. I made an appointment. I went for a consultation; apparently my sister has recently died."

"Oh, I'm so sorry I..."

"No, no, I'm sorry, I shouldn't be flippant about it. I *pretended* I'd lost my sister. She's alive and well down in Kent actually. I used a false name too. The point is that I now know exactly what you mean. The woman is assuredly a fraud. She even suggested to me that my sister might have tried to contact me by telephone, I mean from beyond the grave. It would be funny if it wasn't so serious."

Mary smiled at this. "Well it is a bit funny when you talk about it like that."

Philip was pleased to see her smile.

"Anyway, I am convinced she's a fraud, she's just out to con people. She gave me a heavy hint about making another appointment. As I said, I'm still not sure what can be done, but I very much want to do something. Can you leave it with me a while longer, I'll talk to Miriam – Sergeant Jayne – again now, I'll tell her about my visit and you and I can talk again in due course, that okay?"

Mary nodded with enthusiasm and got up from the table offering thanks.

"No need for a thank you. Not yet, let's see what we can actually do," said Philip "Now, can I line you up with something new to read? I've got the new Ian Rankin under the desk, just come in, you like him don't you? Just don't tell anyone you got it first." Philip's attitude to rules was rather different to that of his predecessor. Sometimes he wondered what she was up to now, he was quite sure that the library functioned better without her brooding presence.

On the way home Philip checked in at Abigail's house. He wanted to make sure all was well there as Mac and Poy's visit came closer. He had had a second estate agent look round the place and would soon have two responses and valuations to show Mac when he arrived in England. He was pleased to have the dates for their visit agreed and he'd arranged to meet Mac and Poy at Heathrow when they flew into England. With the travel arrangements in mind he had been thinking of an idea for himself and Miriam. They had visited Thailand during their search for Michael, a search prompted by Philip's promise to help her just before she died. Although, in part, the trip had been linked to that search and his hope to track down Michael, some of it had been holiday. Miriam had surprised him by joining him on the trip and it was then that they had become close, so close that not only had their room booking changed from single to double but he had also found himself proposing to her on the way home. Neither had been to Thailand before and they both loved the place, they had stayed at nice hotels, first a posh one set alongside the river in Bangkok, the other a small but excellent beach resort in Phuket: chosen to be convenient to the marina where they hoped to find a clue as to what had become of Michael, it had proved to be a real find. The whole trip had all proved to be something of a treat. Mac and Poy had wanted them to stay longer and while that was not possible at the time, they had promised to go back. Philip felt this was too good an opportunity to miss: he would suggest they book another holiday, travel back to Thailand with Mac and Poy and spend some time with them while they were there. There was more to explore in Phuket and they had a standing invitation to go out sailing on Mac's boat again. In the time following the moment his wife had died he had taken no holiday at all until the Mac finding trip, his holiday fund would cover the cost without depleting it. It was a good idea, even if it acted to put what might be called a honeymoon ahead of any wedding arrangements. He wondered what Miriam would make of that, deciding that she would see the logic of it and go along with him; he reckoned more time in Thailand could not fail to appeal.

Philip had left an exercise book on the side in Abigail's living room: it contained all the information he had been checking regarding the sale of the house, from the contact details for the estate agents and for his solicitor to such things as the details of where to get a skip if that proved necessary. Last time he had come in, to show a second estate agent around, he had brought in a carton of milk, so he was able to go into the kitchen and make some tea.

He clicked on the kettle and opened the kitchen cupboard where the mugs were kept. He saw that the one he most often used was not there just as he also took in that there were now two mugs upturned in the plate rack alongside the sink. He was pretty sure that he had made tea for the estate agent on their recent visit, but he was also pretty sure he had put the mugs away. Moving mugs? Again?

"Are you playing games with me Abigail?"

He found that he had spoken the question out loud, while thinking that the more logical explanation was an intruder. Or his memory was faulty, but he was sure, well pretty sure that he had cleared the mugs away. To be sure, he walked round the house, taking his time. All the windows were secure, upstairs and down. No burglars seemed to have visited and he didn't believe in ghosts; his memory must be at fault he decided. He shrugged and returned to the kitchen. He finished his tea, made a note in the book and returned it to the living room and looked back to reassure himself that he had put the mugs he had rinsed and dried back in the cupboard. He could not be sure if anything else in the house had been moved or not, but nothing appeared obviously disturbed.

*

The Library staff meeting broke up with everyone in good spirits. Philip was confident he had changed things for the better since he had taken over from the odious Froby both for staff and members. Previously her meetings, which they all dreaded, had been known as "dofours" on account of their being concerned solely with four things, her telling them: do this, don't do that, you can't do that, (referring to suggestions), and why haven't you done that yet? Her monologues took almost all the available time and her first reaction to anyone daring to chip in was a frown, most often followed by a reason why whatever was said was inappropriate. Philip took a much more consultative view of his role. By and large his small team were all library fans, they enjoyed working there and wanted the place to be good. And they had ideas about it too; all he had to do was prompt them and encourage them. He had noticed that, since Margaret had brought up the subject of the notice board and he had suggested she sort it out, it was always full of interesting stuff and that many regular library users now made a point of looking at it during their visits. It did sometimes prompt some odd messages too, he reflected, thinking of the enigmatic "countdown cards". There had now been four of them: the last one found outside the church. The latest, which he had noticed today, consisted of just two words: TIME PASSES…. He had seen no hint of who might be posting them, but then again he had no idea of what a phantom notice poster looked like. If he could work out what they meant then that might give some clue about the sort of person he was looking for. For the moment it remained a mystery and, he had to admit, an increasingly annoying one. Again he put the card away in his desk drawer and resolved to think more about it later. Various examples of things working well in the library reassured him he was proceeding on the right lines and that Margaret, who had been on the verge of leaving because of Froby's constant put downs, was going to be an excellent member of the little team.

Margaret hung behind as the meeting ended and then asked him:

"What is going on with Mary Donaldson, you did say you'd tell me?" Her look said she expected an answer.

Philip smiled, Margaret, as the youngest and newest of the team, would never have broached an issue like that with his predecessor. It pleased him that she felt she could with him. He was happy to reply.

"Please don't talk about this, Mary is deeply embarrassed about what she did. Anyway after her husband died a friend introduced her to a psychic, they promised she could speak to her husband, but of course she couldn't, it was just a con to get her to pay for the sessions. She feels very silly now that she was taken in. But she's grieving. I'm sure she'll get through it. Meantime I'm checking to see whether there is anything that can be done about what I think amounts to fraud." He didn't mention the paint spraying, balancing Mary's privacy with his efforts to get Margaret more involved in library affairs and feel he was taking her into his confidence. Her first reaction was to express sympathy.

"Oh poor woman. I can't imagine anyone doing that. You asked earlier if I believe in ghosts; well I don't. And I wouldn't want to do anything like that either."

"Well there you are, I said I'd tell you. It's nice if we can help people if they bring their problems into the library, but we also need to respect their privacy too, okay."

Margaret nodded and went back to her work. It would not surprise him if in due course she was asking for an update. He glanced after her for a second as she went back about her work. To start with she had some new items to pin on the notice board.

CHAPTER EIGHT

This is not for everyone

"Perhaps it's an animal: maybe a cat."

Philip had been telling Miriam about the matter of things seeming to move in Abigail's house and, no surprise, she dismissed the idea of ghosts out of hand.

"A cat might move something, I suppose… no, no it couldn't and it certainly couldn't get a mug out of a cupboard or wash it up. Besides how would it get into the house?"

"Maybe it's a ghost cat, you could try leaving it out a saucer of milk, maybe if you did that it would stop trying to make itself a mug of tea!" Miriam grinned as she spoke, it was apparent that she was not taking the problem with the seriousness Philip might have felt it deserved.

The burden of their conversation over breakfast had been about Philip's holiday idea, and Miriam had agreed at once that going back to Thailand and taking a break timed so that they could travel back with Mac and Poy was a great idea. They knew the visit dates now and might even be able to book to go out on the same flight on which their friends were returning. Given how little holiday they had taken in the last couple of years, both of them would be able to organise some leave at comparative short notice. It was agreed.

"The library is closed today," said Miriam, "can I leave flights and so on with you to fix. What are you up to, will you have time?"

"No problem, I've got to go to the library in Chelmsford, but I'm happy to make time for that. I'm just glad you agree. I've got Mac and Poy's return flight details. Are you happy to leave all the arrangements to me?"

"Oh yes, of course, you did a pretty good job last time as I remember… and look what that led to! I don't mind regarding this as the honeymoon, but wedding ideas are with you too though, even if that is going to need to be later, don't forget that?" Miriam smiled again, also adding: "Right, must go now" as she moved to go out and on duty.

Philip had not forgotten about the matter of the wedding, how could he? But he had a number of different things on his mind. He had been torn between telling Miriam about his visit to Jane Wearing and his conviction that she was a fake and his desire to devise something further he could do to create more of what she would regard as evidence first. His sense of fair play and his promise to Mary Donaldson had him resolved to take things further if he could. He *would* tell Miriam in due course, but just not yet.

Meantime he wondered about the detective's business card that the Wearing woman had given him. It seemed an odd thing to do and he wanted to see what was going on. It was Wednesday and the Maldon Library was closed. He still looked back and remembered when a whole day closed mid-week had been regarded as unthinkable; sometimes he thought the world was changing too fast and for the worse, without doubt the financial pressures at the library were greater these days. After some administrative work at his desk, which he sometimes found more convenient to do when the library was not open to the public, it was time to go to the main library in Chelmsford. Maybe, after his time there, he would take steps to see just what sort of detective this Gary Hunt person was. He felt his curiosity was rising.

At the library he spoke with a couple of colleagues and sat at a table in the huge upstairs "Study area" for a while attending to his work. A couple of hours later, his chores at the main library done, he walked along the main street of Chelmsford, a pedestrian-only thoroughfare sometimes home to market stalls. At the end, beyond the river, which flowed in a narrow stream beneath the pavement, he waited at the traffic lights and crossed the main road, the through route for traffic out of the town, and walked into the narrow one-way thoroughfare of Moulsham Street. He held the business card in his hand and counted off the numbers of the premises he passed, at least he tried to; it was surprising how few of the small shops displayed one. But at last he spotted the number he wanted over a door at one side of a small café. Two small signs appeared by the door. One was for an osteopath, which set Philip wondering about their choice of address, one that he imagined had their patients struggling up a flight of stairs with a bad back or whatever before they could get treatment. The other sign, a simple, small brass plate in dire need of a clean, said "Gary Hunt Private - Investigation's" and directed him to the second floor. The unnecessary apostrophe suggested something to Philip about the quality of the business, but he resolved not to make any judgement too soon. Finding the outer door open, he went through and climbed up the two flights of stairs inside.

He had given little thought to what to say to the man once they were face to face. He just wanted to get a feel of what services he offered and, if he discovered that he had acted for Abigail, how that had gone. He had mentioned a missing person to Jane Wearing, so he guessed he should stick with that here too. The top half of the door was opaque glass and it was clear a light was on inside. He knocked and, without waiting for a reply, opened the door.

"Mr Hunt?" He posed the question to a man sitting behind a desk to his left. The desk was heaped with untidy stacks of papers and was home also to a laptop computer, a mug which he presumed contained tea or coffee, an array of pens and pencils standing upright in a pint beer mug and a rather old-fashioned telephone. The rest of the room was furnished in a practical manner, with a filing cabinet in army green, a table against a wall which, like the desk, was covered with papers, and an occasional table alongside which three wooden framed easy chairs were set. The man behind the desk, who made television's Arthur Daley look like an upstanding citizen, was more run down looking than the room. Perhaps, thought Philip, nondescript was the default look in his profession, he did not appear to be a man to whom most people would give a second glance, ideal for tailing people unnoticed perhaps.

"That's me," he replied giving Philip a what-do-you-want sort of look that he supposed it was just possible that he intended to be inviting, but to which he gave insufficient attention to make it work.

"Sorry to arrive unannounced, I was nearby. I may need the help of someone like you, do you have a minute or two to tell me how you work and what costs might be?" At the prospect of a new paying client Hunt became more animated and looked almost interested. He pointed to an upright chair near the desk and Philip sat down

"Depends what it's about," he said, adding: "What is it about?"

"A missing person," replied Philip, "no suspicious circumstances I don't think, just people who have lost touch." He added no more detail, wanting only to get an idea of how the man worked.

"Well, something like that is a bit unpredictable. It usually involves some desk research, and online through the internet these days of course, but it's the visits if there are people to check things out with that take time. I charge an hourly rate and expenses, travel and so on." He named an hourly rate and Philip could at once imagine just how it might mount up.

"I see," he said, "I might have to think about that first."

"Do that by all means, but I recommend you don't wait too long or the trail might get colder, see what I mean?"

"Yes, okay. I'll have to talk to my friend, there is more than one of us involved." He did not feel this was going anywhere. It was apparent that he man was not the Rolls Royce of investigators and Philip would not have been tempted to use him even if he had a real missing person to find.

"Is it important, finding this person?" Hunt was not going to let it go yet.

"Well yes, well to us anyway." Philip couldn't let this go too far without more of a cover story in mind.

"Well, take my card," he burrowed under a pile of paper on his desk, his hand emerging with a box of business cards. He extracted one and passed it over. Philip took it as he responded:

"I have a card actually," he took it out of his pocket and held it up. "That's how I know your name. But it's from way back. I believe you did some work for a lady called Abigail Croft, she lived in Maldon, but it would have been some twenty years back. Do you remember?"

"Name doesn't ring a bell, but it wouldn't after so long, right? I suppose I could look it up." He rose and came out from behind the desk and moved towards the filing cabinet, which Philip now saw had its drawers marked with the letters of the alphabet. He burrowed in the top drawer, marked A – D, extracted a slim file and returned to his seat and opened it up.

"Yes," he said, "Annabel Croft. I appear to have tried to find her son, Michael." Philip noted that he had her name wrong, but it sounded as if it was Abigail. He did not mention it.

"But, you didn't, find him I mean. In fact he only turned up recently after Abigail died. He had gone to Thailand. Lived there ever since." He resisted saying anything about his involvement and his detective work having been successful.

"Right. Well that's how it goes sometimes if there was no sign of where he had gone, it was unlikely that anyone would notice him if he was as far away as that either."

No further comment was made on either side while Philip thought that the file, which appeared to contain a mere couple of sheets of paper, did not seem to indicate a very thorough investigation and it seemed to Philip that Abigail had not got value for money or even had got so little that she had been ripped off. Hunt returned to the present and continued:

"Take this too," he said and gave Philip another business card. Philip saw it was for Jane Wearing. "Just an idea," he went on, "this is not for everyone and it's no alternative to the thorough investigation I can undertake, but this lady is uncanny. She might come up with the very clue that leads us to your man. Is it a man you're looking for, incidentally?"

"Yes, it is." Philip had no idea why he had gone with that, he must, he thought present a coherent picture, and he went on "but a psychic, I wonder if..." Hunt interrupted him:

"I know, sounds daft, and I remember thinking that too once, but, well the proof is in the results isn't it?"

Philip stood up, determined to finish the encounter.

"I suppose so, anyway, let me give it all some thought, I'll talk to my friend and get back to you. A day or two, eh?"

"Up to you" said Hunt and tapped a cigarette out of a packet retrieved from under another pile of paper. The man was a fire and health hazard, thought Philip. He expressed brief thanks and took his leave before the room filled with smoke.

Outside the office two figures blocked his way as they sat on the stairs. Two scruffy young men in jeans and hoodies were conferring together and hearing the door above open they both pushed something into their pockets and stood up, one slipping down the stairs and out into the street, the other heading past Philip making no attempt to avoid brushing against him on the narrow stairs, and going straight into Hunt's office without knocking. Someone he knew then, thought Philip, reflecting that it looked rather likely that he had just witnessed a drug purchase. What that said about Hunt, he rather wondered.

Downstairs he walked a few more doors along Moulsham Street and went into another café. There was without doubt a link between Jane Wearing and this man; it was clear they recommended each other and might even work together in other ways for all Philip knew. He was relieved he had not mentioned how he had got Hunt's name from Jane Wearing or the facts might not have come out in the same way. It seemed more like a collaboration than a coincidence and one that, at least from Philip's perspective, seemed designed to make it easier for the pair to make money from the likes of Mary Donaldson. What else the man might be into Philip did not know.

"What can I get you?" Philip was startled for a second: he had been standing at the café counter, but his mind had been miles away.

"Sorry, just a tea please." A moment later he carried it to a table and sat down; he had some thinking to do.

There were various things on his mind: Mac and Poy's impending visit, a holiday, wedding ideas, he couldn't forget that, Jane Wearing, the expanding role he intended for Margaret in the library, but he dismissed Hunt. It seemed that Abigail had used him to search for Mac, he just hoped she had not spent too much money with him; he seemed to Philip to be of dubious character and uncertain effectiveness. Still Mac might be interested in the fact that Abigail's search for him had been that thorough, she had not let him go easily. He must remember to tell him about it, he thought, they would be on their way to England soon.

CHAPTER TEN

I thought she wouldn't mind

Philip still puzzled about recent events at Abigail's house. He was sure that things had moved. He was certain of this and he was just as sure it wasn't a ghost, especially not a ghostly cat. It remained an enigma. This time, the moment Philip entered through the front door he knew at once that something was wrong, and it certainly wasn't a trespassing cat. For a start the house was warm, it felt as if the heating was full on, and he was sure he had turned it down very low just to keep the empty house from getting chilly and damp, more important, so was the kettle. He could hear it bubbling away in the kitchen. It seemed that the mug mover was in the house. He stood still for a moment, closed the front door behind him, careful not to make a noise, thought for a moment about looking for a weapon, though he had heard Miriam talking about what constituted "reasonable force" on one occasion and wondered what was appropriate, anyway Abigail was not the type to keep a baseball bat in her hall stand, and he would have no idea at all how hard to hit anyone with it even if he got the chance. He didn't appear to have been heard, any noise his entering the house had made being covered by the bubbling of the kettle, which sounded as if it was just coming to the boil, so, with no real further thought but now decisive, he strode through the hall unarmed and pushed open the kitchen door. Inside a figure moved fast from the worktop towards the back door and he paused, worried by the thought of an intruder, but then he saw it was a child. He shouted and the boy, having failed to get the key unlocked in time to effect an escape turned towards him.

"Terry Walsh!" Philip said in amazement recognising the lad at once. "What are you doing here, how did you get in and…" He paused, lost for words and wondering what to say next.

"Sorry." The boy looked sheepish and cast his eyes down but he offered no explanation and his dejected expression seemed to foretell no threat.

"Are you stealing?" Philip asked yet feeling the thought was absurd, the boy appeared to be making a cup of tea; a leisurely steal perhaps.

The question brought an immediate denial: "No, no… well I borrowed some money, it was on the kitchen table, for the milkman… I didn't think Aunt Abigail would mind, well she can't now can she, but well anyway…" He tailed off.

Philip was now even more confused. Aunt? He'd said aunt.

"You knew Abigail Croft?" He queried, watching the boy's face, but it suggested no sign of a lie.

"Yes." He said, but offered no explanation, just adding "She died." Philip registered that he knew about that and changed tack; having been the one who found her body he still found he was a little uncomfortable dwelling on her death.

"Were you making tea?" He asked and Terry nodded. Philip took in the carton of milk sitting on the side and noticed too that there were a few dishes in the sink.

"Make a cup for us both and we'll sit down and talk, I think we need to get to the bottom of this, don't you?"

Terry was silent, but he turned back to the worktop, clicked the kettle back on and got a second mug out of the cupboard and added a teabag from the jar. When the kettle had boiled again he made two mugs, spilling a little milk as he added it and thus demonstrating his nervousness. A minute of two later they were sitting opposite each other at the kitchen table with Philip trying to decide what to do, what to ask first.

"Why are you here?" Terry asked, his nervousness clear in his face, speaking first, perhaps to fill the silence.

"I was a friend of Abigail's," Philip replied, wondering for a second why this was starting with him explaining himself to Terry, though it had got a conversation under way.

"I'm getting the house ready for sale, her son arrives soon. He lives overseas." He stopped, it was a reasonable question, Terry doubtless did wonder what he was doing there, but the explanation seemed to satisfy him and he remained silent again. Philip reckoned his finding out about Terry was the most important thing.

"Does your mother know you're here?" He thought this was a suitable starting point and hoped for a quick explanation. But Terry's reaction was to start to cry: a tear ran down his cheek and he sniffed hard, as he attempted not to show his level of upset, and reached into his pocket for a handkerchief. He may have reached an age where appearing grown up was important to him, but the situation he was in was extreme.

He had dreaded this moment… he wiped his face to give himself a moment to think, then started to speak. He rejected telling a lie, he remembered Jackson nagging him and he knew he had to tell someone about his situation.

"Mum's gone away," he said. Once he had begun speaking it all came out in a rush: his mother's unexpected vanishing and his attempts to keep going alone; the growing problems, food, money, and the electricity. And his gaining entrance to Abigail's house.

"I couldn't think of anything else to do," he finished. He had no real idea what he wanted to happen next, but he knew he wanted something to happen, something different. Something to sort things out.

"So your Mum hasn't been home for a while" Philip began to try to get the story straight in his mind.

"Yeah, it's weeks." Terry sniffed again as he continued, "she just went, one day I got back from school and she wasn't there. I just thought it was, like, well her, you know, she has depression… ever since my dad left and worse since she lost her job."

"But why ever didn't you tell someone?" Philip found that mystifying, the lad had evidently been living alone for weeks, not, if he was to be believed, breaking into Abigail's house until a day or two back when he no longer had electricity at home.

"I know I should have," Terry looked sheepish. "But I kept thinking she would be home any moment. Once I hadn't said anything for a while, well, then I didn't know how to. Or who to tell. I nearly told a teacher, I nearly told you the other day in the library, you'll help won't you Mr M? I've been so frightened."

"Why frightened? For your mother?" Philip asked.

"Yes, I suppose so, but I've always assumed she's fine… wherever she's gone, I mean what else can it be, she's just gone off to be quiet, like when she shuts herself in her bedroom for days." He blinked back tears and Philip began to realise just how upset he was.

"But I was frightened for me. They'll take me into care, I'd hate that." He made the words sound like he was referring to the undead and the phrase "take me into care" seem like one that described his very worst nightmare. He ended with a pleading tone "Will you help? Please will you help?" and another sniff.

"Well, let's see." Philip thought for a moment. It was apparent that something had to be done, the lad couldn't just go on this way, and besides quite apart from Terry there was the question of Mrs Walsh. What had happened to her?

"Have you told me everything?" he asked, "you've no idea where your Mum is, you've managed on your own at home until the electricity went out, then you broke in here. Is that right?"

"It didn't seem like that, not really breaking in, it's Aunt Abigail's house, my Dad did the garden in their old house; you know way back before her husband died. She kept in touch with Mum after Dad left. I thought she wouldn't mind, but…" Terry's voice tailed off.

"Okay, and you promise you haven't stolen anything" Philip paused and waited for Terry to answer.

"I borrowed the milk money, just borrowed, Mum will pay it back when she comes home. And I took the books she got me about sailing."

"Sailing?" Philip queried.

"Yes, I sail with a friend and the school has a link with one of the local sailing clubs, I've done a bit, it's great. I want to learn more and the school lets groups attend training courses at the club in the summer. Aunt Abigail got me a couple of books. It was a while ago, I forgot about it after I heard she'd died. I saw the books in the living room, I knew they were for me, so there was no harm, sorry…" He tailed off again, though he was looking a bit better now; he seemed to be relieved to have got everything out in the open at last.

"Anything else I should know?" Terry got up and turned to the worktop beyond the kettle and brought some books back to the table.

"These are the sailing books, but this is different", a brown envelope with a photo stuck to the front with a paper clip lay on the table. "That's my Dad, I think it's taken in the Croft's old garden." The man in the photo was standing by a wooden arch covered in a profusion of flowers that had climbed to the top. Philip was no gardener, he did not know what the plants were, but the man appeared to be displaying them with pride. It didn't surprise him that Abigail's old family home had a well-tended garden; her husband was well off and working in London as he had, it was logical that he could have had help in what appeared to be a large garden.

"That's it?"

"Yes. I opened the envelope, but there was money inside. I knew not to take that and stuck it down again."

Terry fell silent and Philip looked at the envelope. It was self-sealing and showed signs of having been opened, losing some of its original adhesion in the process. But that, he decided, would have to wait, as he suddenly realised how much time had gone by, he'd promised Miriam he would be home by this time. He had popped in to check something the estate agent needed to complete the house sales details, he had intended it to be a matter of a few minutes. Besides it also occurred to him that he was alone in someone else's house with a young boy aged thirteen or fourteen, something that in this day and age could be interpreted as suspicious rather than helpful.

"Well, let's try and sort you out, shall we?" Terry looked at him with soulful eyes, his hair, which was overdue to be cut flopping into them.

"Come on we'll go and consult the long arm of the law." He meant it in a jocular way, a reference to Miriam who was waiting for him at home, but Terry's face changed in a moment and he went wide eyed.

"No, no, I'm sorry, it wasn't really breaking in. I was only…"

Philip interrupted him before he could go any further. "Sorry Terry, I am not going to march you to the police station and get you arrested for breaking and entering, I meant, well… my fiancé is a police officer, you know, Sergeant Jayne. It's just that she deals with things like this, she'll know what to do and she'll be able to help you. Let's lock up safe here shall we, do bring the books. I live just along the road, that's how I knew Abigail. Come on."

Philip couldn't imagine quite what the next step should be, he avoided even thinking the phrase "taken into care", but he knew that getting Terry cared for was the main priority.

They walked along the road until they arrived at Philip's front door. Inside he gave his usual call of "Anyone there?" to be answered by Miriam's response of "What time do you call this then? You were supposed to be getting supper." Philip added, "Sorry I'm late, and, well it may have to be fish and chips now. But come and say hello, we've got a guest."

"So who's here then?" she asked coming into the living room from the kitchen holding a tea cloth.

"It's Terry, Terry Walsh, I think I've mentioned him to you, he's one of my regular library users. He lives just up the road and he's got a bit of a problem." Well, more than a bit of one in fact he thought.

"Well, I'll have to leave it with you for the moment, I was just writing you a note, I've got to go out, a bit of an emergency, I'm afraid. I ate some cheese and biscuits while I waited for you. I'll leave you two to it, don't wait up Philip, I may be late… and sorry, but I must rush. Nice to see you Terry." She smiled at the boy, but moved on with no time for conversation.

Used by now to the unpredictable demands of police work, Philip let Miriam go without comment, she gave him a peck on the cheek as she went towards the front door. Then he was on his own with Terry and his problems. He started with something practical, explaining that it seem best for Terry to sleep with them that night, and walked him upstairs and showed him the spare bedroom.

"Bathroom's that door there." He pointed. Philip led the way back to the living room and sat down to collect his thoughts. He realised that he was still clutching the envelope Terry had given him in the house.

"Let's see what we've got here, sit you down." He opened the envelope and pulled out the contents, finding and counting out sixty five pounds in notes. Terry had said he had not touched this. Also inside was a few sheets of paper. On top was a page torn out from Abigail's journal. Philip recognised her handwriting; he had found journals in her house soon after her death and found information in them that had prompted what had become his somewhat obsessive search for her son Michael.

"There are pages here from her journal. I found more of this after she died. Let's see what it says." It quickly became clear what this page was about as he read out loud what she had written:

It's some year since the Walsh family split up. Mr Walsh always seemed nice enough, he certainly kept our garden in good order. There is apparently no clue to why he's left, his wife doesn't know where he's gone or if it's to be with someone else, that's the commonest thing isn't it?

Anyway I have to find someone else to help with the garden now. He evidently made it clear he was leaving, he took things with him and his wife said it looked like he had somewhere else to go, certainly he made it clear he was leaving her and had no intention of coming back.

"That must have been written years ago" said Philip. A second page and entry followed on and was written a little later. He read on from a second sheet.

Saw Mrs Walsh today. She's clearly been struggling a bit since her husband walked out. She has a young boy to take care of too. I said he could visit. I'll keep in touch and try to keep an eye on him.

The next sheet was torn from a notebook. At the top there was written a single word: *Terry* followed by a date which Philip assumed was Terry's birthday as she had also written *Send card and book*. A final piece of paper, a quite recent one it appeared, listed the titles of two books about sailing, which might well, thought Philip, be the ones Terry had just taken from the house. It seemed clear that Abigail had not only resolved to keep an eye on the boy but that she had done so, also ending up living in the same road when she had moved after her husband had died. The envelope appeared to be designed to act as a prompt to her to keep in touch with Terry.

"Did Abigail used to give you a birthday card?" He asked.

"Yes, a present too, why?" Terry looked puzzled at the question.

"Well, that envelope you found seems to have been a reminder to remember the date and keep in touch. When's your birthday?" Terry told him the date and Philip confirmed it was the same as the one in Abigail's note.

"This not only shows you did know her, but you should know that she wanted to keep an eye on you. I think the money in the envelope – there was £65.00 – was a bit of a float to buy you the odd thing, like a card and a present on your birthday. That's nice isn't it?"

"It was always a book," said Terry referring to the birthday presents. "I didn't see much of her, but yes, she was always kind to me."

"I'll ask Michael about the money when he comes, seems to me it ought to go to you." He left the matter there and continued changing the subject.

"Okay now Terry, what about some food. Fish and chips do alright?" Terry nodded. "I'll walk round and get some, you go and get some things from home so that you have what you need to sleep here tonight and we'll need to sort your situation out tomorrow when Miriam can get involved. Is that okay?" He didn't wait for an answer adding "And leave a note saying where you are, just in case it's now your Mum comes back." Terry nodded, and they both headed out.

When Miriam came back late in the evening both Philip and Terry were in bed sound asleep. A note on the kitchen table explained. Philip had made up the bed in the spare room and then the two of them had spent an hour or two eating and chatting, Philip trying to offer reassurance to Terry though without getting too much further, after all he didn't know how these things worked, it seemed to him that nothing could be done now late in the evening but they had agreed to put matters to Miriam when they could all get together the following day.

A little before that could happen, however, Miriam was to give Philip something of a shock.

CHAPTER ELEVEN

Procedures to be gone through

"Whatever were you thinking?" Miriam's face was like thunder. It was not an expression Philip was yet used to, in their months together they had had words very little, a few minor disagreements, naturally enough, but nothing serious. This was in a different league and all the more daunting because of that, Philip found he had no idea what he had done to deserve it, which made it even more mystifying.

"What do you…?" But Philip didn't get to finish his question as Miriam continued apace.

"This boy is a minor, a vulnerable minor, and his mother appears to be a missing person. Something needs to be done. Quickly. At once. Where is he now?"

"Terry went to school as usual. I was only trying to help. We'd agreed to talk to you about it all after Terry got back from school today." Philip had felt that what had occurred was little different in nature from many a helpful conversation he had with library users during the day. At least it had started out that way; now he was being forced to see his actions in a rather different way.

"Okay, I'm sure you were only being helpful, but leave it with me now, will you? I'll get something moving, there are procedures you know. I'll be home about six, we can talk then, okay?"

"Okay, fine" Philip's voice now had a sheepish edge and Miriam saw his distress. Her expression softened; after all she had no doubt of his good intentions.

"Don't worry, I'm sure no harm's been done, we'll sort it out. Don't worry, I'll see you later."

Philip had told Miriam about Terry in the morning. But Miriam had been a little late up after a late night on duty and Terry had already gone out, heading off to school, before they could cross paths and talk face to face. Once Miriam had left and having had time to think about things, Philip did realise that he had perhaps acted without due consideration, but it had been a shock finding someone in Abigail's house and then he had recognised Terry, someone he knew, and then it had just gone on from there. He was confident, however, that Miriam would know what to do next and how to sort things out. Thinking that there was no more that he could do for the moment at least he headed off to the library.

As he walked along the High Street little did he know that as the day went on he would find that what was already a somewhat difficult situation, had taken a distinct turn for the worse.

There were aspects of Philip's job that were just downright tedious. But they had to be done, Froby's nonsensible memos apart, and he was meticulous in keeping the necessary paperwork up to date; if only so that he could get it out of the way allowing him to concentrate on what he saw as more important matters. The importance of finances were increasing too and there was planning and checking needed on that front. This morning he had decided to have an "admin hour" as he described such times to his team. But his mind was elsewhere and then, almost as soon as he had sat down, he jumped up. Terry, he thought. What about Terry? Leaving matters to Miriam was fine, she was qualified to know what to do, but he couldn't have a policeman turning up at the school unannounced and unexpected after all he had said to Terry, especially after what he had discovered about Abigail and Terry's family. It would frighten the lad no end, and worse he would think that Philip had set them on him behind his back; and indeed, he thought, that might then be pretty much the truth of the matter.

He rushed out of his office to find the library going quietly about its business and had a very brief word with one of his colleagues who was on duty at the front desk.

"Sorry, sudden emergency," he said, "I have to pop out, just for a few minutes. Back very soon. Tell the others, okay?"

"Fine I'll..." they began a reply, but Philip was gone. The admin would have to wait.

The library was situated alongside the car park and it was a mere couple of hundred metres away round the corner from there to the school. It took Philip only a matter of a few minutes to hurry round there; a chilly walk as he had not paused to put on anything warm. He knew the school secretary, he had done a good few talks at the school over the years, and she smiled a greeting when he reached her office, adding:

"Hello, this is an unexpected visit, what can I do for you?"

In as few rushed words as possible he explained to her that he needed to see Terry Walsh. She hesitated, there were protocols to be born in mind here. So she began by giving him a spiel about how he wasn't a relative and that regulations didn't permit just anyone to turn up at the school and have access to the children, but the look on Philip's face, his insistence that it was important and a little more hasty explanation of the circumstances seemed to be sufficient for her to change her mind.

"Alright. Give me a minute, I'll bring him here, if we see him together we should be fine, will that be okay?"

"Yes of course, but please hurry. No one else has asked for him this morning have they?"

"No." Again Philip's look seemed to be enough to drive her on and prevent further enquiry. She left the room promising to be back in a few minutes. It seemed like an age as he waited and Philip walked to and fro in the small office; prowling up and down, though he had been relieved to find that it seemed he had arrived in time to stop an unexpected police visit being a surprise. After about five minutes, during which time Philip imagined Terry being located and escorted through the labyrinthine corridors of the much extended old school building, the secretary returned with Terry at her side. Despite having had time to think about it, Philip struggled to know quite what to say as Terry spoke up first.

"Hello. Thanks so much Mr. M, you really helped me last night."

They all sat down and Philip collected his thought and began.

"Well, I'm glad if things are out in the open and we can perhaps sort everything out for you now. But Miriam wasn't happy at all. You'd gone when she got up, but she told me in no uncertain terms that there were procedures to follow and she made me leave the next move to her. She'll sort things out for you, I'm sure. I don't know exactly what will happen next, but I suddenly realised that you might find the police arriving to see you here at school today and wonder what was going on."

"I don't want… well you know, but I guess things need sorting. Are you out of it now Mr M?" Philip gave it just a moment's thought.

"Well. Yes. No, I'll do whatever I can. Tell them we know each other, tell them I need to be kept informed and we'll see. Miriam will give me the details in due course, I'm pretty sure she'll come herself. But you're right, things do need sorting out. Try not to worry, okay? I just didn't want anything happening without you knowing about it." But of course, neither of them really knew how things would be handled. Nevertheless Philip reassured Terry as best he could.

"You really could not be in better hands. Miriam will look after you, she knows what must be done, you know for you and your mother, and she'll make sure that your best interests are put first. Besides, who knows, your mother might come home at any moment and then all this will be unnecessary."

"Alright, I suppose. Thanks for coming in." Terry did not look exactly happy, but Philip hoped he had been able to reassure him to some extent, certainly so that he did not feel Philip had been inappropriately going behind his back in light of their previous conversations.

Philip promised him that they would speak again soon, he thanked the secretary and watched as she went off to see Terry on his way back to class. He walked back to the library, hurrying to get back to his desk, at that moment he did not realise just how much help Terry might need.

It was almost break time when Terry re-joined the class and the second the bell sounded, echoing along the corridors, he went to talk to Jackson, who had earlier watched him escorted from the class with no explanation and, knowing the difficulties, had wondered what was happening to his friend.

"What goes on?" he said then continuing in a lower, more confidential tone "has your Mum come home yet?"

"No" said Terry. "But I followed your advice, J, I told someone. I'd got into Aunt Abigail's empty house, you know just along the road, it's got the electric on and I could charge my phone and… you know. Anyway Mr M., you know who I mean, from the library, caught me there – they were friends, since she died he's been helping to get the house ready for sale. Her son lives somewhere overseas, he's coming home to get it all done." J contemplated asking how he got into a locked house but, concentrating on what happened next, he posed another question.

"So, you told him everything?"

"Yes, then he gave me a meal and I stayed at his house last night. His fiancé's a police Sergeant, she knows what to do and is getting things organised. That's why I was called out, J., Mr M came to tell me someone will come and see me later. I'm dead worried."

"You'll be okay. They sound like they'll be on your side." The bell ringing again interrupted them and they headed off back to class again.

"Tell me what happens, and if you are rushed to prison, text me!" Jackson said, grinning at his choice of parting shot. Despite his fears Terry found the friendly banter was sort of comforting and smiled back.

Clare Townsend had worked at the local council for some fifteen years. She was responsible for various aspects of child welfare and had a motherly look to match. She was what Alistair McCall Smith's wonderful lady detective would call "traditionally built", though if her weight should ever be commented on, it would doubtless be in a "fat and jolly" sort of way. Just arrived, she sat down at her desk in Chelmsford's County Hall facing a cup of coffee, a full in-tray and an array of message notes on sticky yellow sheets, her coat was unbuttoned but still on as she took a few moments to warm up after the journey to work. Before she could take off her coat or look at her messages, the telephone on her desk rang and several different long strings of beads in clashing colours clattered together as she leant forward across the desk to pick it up and spoke her name.

"Morning Clare. It's Sergeant Jayne." The two women had crossed paths before, knew each other a little and, while not quite friends, got on well.

"Hello. How are you? And how can I help?" asked Clare, assuming the call had a business purpose.

"I'm fine, thanks, but I've a bit of a problem." In a few words Miriam explained about Terry being left on his own and the events of the previous evening.

"Could you meet me at the school? Soon, please." They made the arrangement. Clare would phone once she had got clear and had driven over to Maldon. Miriam's procedures to be gone through were now very much under way.

After Clare's drive to Maldon and the promised phone call had been made, the two met up as planned. The secretary at the school had found them an office to use and had gone to get Terry from his class. In normal circumstances Miriam would have checked out the situation first before calling in Social Services, but the information she had from Philip was, she was sure, reliable, and there was of course some urgency involved. One meeting with both she and Clare seeing Terry would do it.

"He'll probably be glad to miss a bit of maths," said Clare as they sat waiting, but she was only filling the silence and remembering her own school days, she had enough experience to know the lad would in all likelihood assume the worst of her visit; at the very least he would be confused and worried.

"I'll start if that's okay" said Miriam "I did meet Terry, very briefly, last night and once my bit's done I can leave you to it." The secretary returned as she spoke and seated Terry at a third chair.

"Just tell them all about it, Terry, they'll help you," she said as she left them to it. Miriam took in Terry's expression, he looked apprehensive, yet maybe she detected relief showing in his face as well.

"Hello again Terry, sorry I rushed off last night. Anyway we need to sort you out, don't we?"

"Suppose." Terry looked glum. "Mr M. said you'd help… I just haven't known what to do."

"Okay, well this is Clare Townsend she's here to help too. Let's start at the beginning, shall we? You live on your own with your Mum, right, how long has she been away?" J was right thought Terry, he needed to tell someone, and he found he trusted Miriam. She was being business-like about it, but it seemed apparent to him that she cared too.

"Two weeks, no nearly three, I think." Piece by piece his story came out. There wasn't really that much to tell: his mother had vanished with no warning, her depression, his carrying on assuming she would be back soon, then it becoming more difficult, the food, the money, and then the additional problem of the electricity.

"I can't even charge my phone," he said, but he said nothing about breaking into another house, though he did wondered if Philip had told her about that. Miriam made some notes and then made to pass the conversation over to Clare. Nothing was said about his house breaking activities.

"Okay. I'll let Clare go through things with you in a moment," she said. "But I must make some enquiries about your Mum, we need to find out where she is, make sure she's alright, okay? We'll start at the house. Can I borrow your house keys for a little while? I'll see if I can find any clues and I'll get them back to you via Clare. What number do you live at?" Terry gave her the number, felt in his blazer pocket and produced his house keys. Miriam took the keys, told him she would see him again soon and encouraged him not to worry.

"Clare will see you right," she said making it sound as if she was sure it was true. Clare acknowledged Miriam's departure, smiled at him and began to ask him some more questions. She started with the basics:
"How old are you Terry?"

Some people just want to disappear and they do just that. They do not want to be found and sometimes they never are traced. But if a missing person report is followed up, it is standard practice to search their home; many a missing person has been found just to be hiding. In addition, sometimes there is evidence found there that promptly identifies where someone has gone, something like the receipt for a rail ticket perhaps, something that rules out foul play and leads to the person being located without problem. So, a little later, when Miriam visited the Walsh home with a constable, they both knew the form. She opened the front door with Terry's keys, picking up some post lying on the mat as they went in. The ground floor flat was cold without electricity, and so the lights didn't work just as Terry had said, but it was daylight and looking around was no problem. Terry had kept the place pretty tidy, there was no huge pile of dirty dishes in the sink and in due course Miriam found the last clothes he had washed were hung in neat rows on a rack in the bathroom.

But, despite a systematic tour through the flat, nothing gave them any immediate clue as to what had happened or where Terry's Mum had gone. Miriam found a battered address book by the telephone and put that in her bag; thinking that maybe that would lead them to someone who knew Mrs Walsh's whereabouts. She then tried the back door. It was locked and there was no key in it; Terry had kept that in his pocket when she had met him at the school earlier thinking he did not want to be without a means of entry.

"You can get into the garden round the side, John, nip out and check the shed will you." She knew to be thorough: it was routine procedure. John went towards the front door and she turned back to a pile of post and papers on the kitchen counter and began to thumb through them, at once finding a red envelope from the utility company that seemed to explain the lack of electricity. Nothing else there seemed to offer a clue and there was little amongst the post anyway apart from circulars. Then she heard a cry and the unmistakable sound of retching in the garden. She looked out through the kitchen window. The shed door stood open and her constable was outside it leaning over a flower bed. It seemed he had found Mrs Walsh.

Without delay she went outside and followed him round the house to confirm the situation and, having done so, spoke a few words to the constable.

"Don't worry, John, it is always difficult the first time. Take a minute, I'll call it in."

Then she reached for her radio to set various other procedures in progress. As she did so she found her mind considering Terry's situation, the poor lad she thought sighing out loud, it seemed his young life was about to change radically.

CHAPTER TWELVE

Where you'll be looked after

Amongst the various formal procedures now set in train Miriam found time to telephone Philip, who she knew had been at the library since first thing, with the news. She updated him, setting out the bald facts to him in a succinct business-like manner.

"Yes looks like suicide, I don't think there's any doubt," she said. "Though there will need to be a post mortem - probably two or three weeks ago – yes, not nice at all – in the garden shed, well a sort of summer house – that's why Terry knew nothing about it, I don't suppose he ever went out there, not in this winter weather – No, Clare Townsend, she's the social worker on the case, will do everything that's necessary for Terry – I've told her the situation, part of the procedure."

"Well I'm so sorry. What a shame. But I guess Terry will be looked after. Poor you too, you do have to deal with some ghastly stuff sometimes don't you?" Philip felt concern for both Terry and Miriam.

"Luckily it's not all bad, but yes, I suppose…" she paused, the sight of Mrs Walsh's body slumped in the chair with the floor below her bloody and, this stuck in her mind, her face covered in cobwebs, still fresh in her mind, then continued "sorry, must go, there's still a good deal to do on this. I'll see you later." Miriam ended the somewhat hurried call leaving Philip contemplating the harsh realities of life, marvelling at how well Miriam seemed to cope with what could be a difficult job and wondering what would now become of Terry in the future. Philip tried to put the matter out of his mind and concentrate, but it would not be long before his phone rang again.

Clare Townsend was well used to circumstances in which people were left bereaved, or left suffering from many other different difficulties too. She met people whose lives had been threatened or ruined in all sorts of ways, ranging from illness to financial trouble and much more besides. Sometimes she could not do other than consider that the circumstances they found themselves in were, in whole or part, their own fault. Bereavement was not often in that category, and the fallout from a death often went way beyond grief, leaving much to be sorted out as one way of life had to supersede another. Generally speaking she coped and coped well, but such things never became routine, never became easy, and this was especially so in a case where children were concerned.

She was used to delivering bad news and always did so in a manner she hoped would soften the blow, whilst knowing full well that doing so was to a very great extent impossible and that she was unleashing a variety of woes as she broke the news. Sometimes she struggled not to let her own upset show. Since he had spoken out, since Philip and Miriam – and the police – had got involved Terry had realised that his mother might not just be hiding away; that something worse was a real possibility. Something more permanent. He had tried not to dwell on such worse possibilities and continued his mind-set of "she'll be back soon", but as soon as he had sat down with Clare it was clear from her serious face that all was not well.

"Terry, I'm afraid…" Those two little words were enough. He knew then with crushing certainty that it was bad news. He listened as she continued, but could still not take in what had happened completely. He asked no questions, she was gone, she had taken her own life. That was enough for the moment, his own fears made him worry more about the "what next?" questions rather than the "why" ones.

As Clare faced him he now seemed to look younger to her. Terry had been silent and withdrawn following what she had had to tell him about his mother. She knew it was the shock, he had gone through the last weeks convincing himself that his mother's absence was just one of those things, that it would all be alright soon and that, wherever she was, his mother was fine and that both she and normality would return soon. Now, whatever his other feelings, he would be worried about himself and what would now happen to him. She did not want to press him but she had to lay out something about the arrangements. No sooner had she started to explain something of what would happen next when Terry became animated.

"I don't want to be taken into care," he said. "I might be sent anywhere, what about my friends, what about…" The words poured out in a rush, then the animation died, his voice tailed off and his face looked … the word that came most readily to Clare's mind was hunted. Almost overnight his world had doubtless seemed to crash out of control.

"Please don't worry," Clare lent forward a little, her necklaces rattling as she did so. "A care order is for when things are really bad, it's designed to protect young people from violence and such like. There is no problem like that here, what's happened is terrible in a different way of course, but we just need to find you somewhere to live, people to live with, foster parents, a new home and family. That's my job now, to find somewhere where you will not only be looked after, but where you'll be happy too." The first job was to organise emergency care, literally from today onwards, then something more permanent. Terry appeared to accept the overall situation, but didn't want to hear about the details. Not now, not yet.

"Can I go back to class now?" he said. He was upset yet still craved normality.

"We'll see. You can't stay alone in your own home tonight, Terry, you must understand that. But I'll have an emergency arrangement made by the time you finish school today. If you're sure you want to stay here for the rest of the day, that is." In many ways she felt it didn't seem right that he went back to class, but all the alternatives Clare could think of would be just as unpleasant for him. For the moment, as he gave her a firm nod, she avoided any argument and agreed with him, trying as she did so to add reassurance.

"Yes. Okay, you'll be with friends, right?"

Terry could think of nowhere else he wanted to be, not brooding on his own somewhere for sure. Besides he wanted to speak to someone he knew, a friend: first choice J. Then he had an idea.

"Yes. Yes, I will. So where I go first is temporary, while you fix something better, right?"

"Not better Terry, just more permanent, all those who undertake fostering are caring. Not just anyone can do it, you know. One of my jobs is checking people out. It's a very thorough process I can assure you. I promise you'll be fine. I'll see you at the end of the day and take you there myself. And if you find you can't face staying in school today, just ask in the office here and I'll come back, okay?" Clare was doing her best, but Terry was intent on pursuing his idea and had another question for her.

When Philip answered the phone Clare Townsend introduced herself and told him that she had been speaking to Terry. Philip knew her name from Miriam, but wondered what she wanted from him.

"I've told Terry how things are," she went on. "We have to find him emergency accommodation, then the fostering system proper will take over and he'll be found a permanent placement. But he's terrified of going 'into care' as he puts it, he sees it as frightening and as perhaps removing him from everything he knows. I'm pretty sure that's why he said nothing to anyone about his mother being missing, he was frightened of what would happen to him if she was away for any length of time."

"I agree. He's a good kid, I hope he'll be alright."

"I'm sure he will be. I'll make sure he is. Meantime he's bearing up well and... he's had an idea. He was adamant about it, and I said I would put it to you." She paused for a moment before continuing: "He wonders if he could stay longer with you and Miriam, you know, just while we get something more permanent organised. He knows you. Clearly he feels safe with you and you live right on his old doorstep too. I know it's an imposition and perhaps I shouldn't ask, but it would be a manageable first step for him and, as I say, he's terrified of where he might end up. It would only be for a few days." Clare paused a beat or two, then added: "what do you think?"

Philip could imagine how awful Terry must be feeling, he did not know him that well, but he imagined any known face was better than a complete stranger and his being put who knew where. They lived in the same road, for Terry getting to school and so on could continue much like before and he would be able to access his stuff at home with no difficulty. His instinct was to help, he had experienced a happy childhood, with no major traumas along the way, and he felt for Terry; he was in a horrid situation. But, of course, it was not a decision he could take alone.

"I suppose, if it's just temporary, we could do that. I should ask Miriam first though, I must. Can I call you back?" She gave him her mobile phone number and they agreed to speak again soon.

Philip didn't like phoning Miriam when she was on duty and working, indeed he knew she would often not answer and so he did it except in special circumstances; that situation was understood between them, it went with the territory, as it were.

This time when her mobile rang and she saw that it was Philip calling, she kind of assumed it was about Terry and took the call.

"Hi, sorry to interrupt, it's about Terry."

"No problem, I'm on a break. Most of the arrangements I need to make are now in train, you know, with the coroner and so on."

"Right." Philip told her about his conversation with Clare and put Terry's request to her. There was a silence on the line just for a moment, then she replied:

"Well, it's only temporary, I guess, but it would be a responsibility. We are both a little erratic in our comings and goings, but he's not that young, he can certainly get to school on his own, right? I know nothing about kids, well a little about bad ones perhaps, but we'll cope I'm sure. If you're happy, okay, do tell her yes."

"Okay I'll do that" said Phillip, he was a little surprised at Miriam's reaction, but pleased also. He had an instinct to help people as did Miriam too, as her pitching into the hunt for Abigail's long lost son – and her job – had shown. Anyway he liked Terry; it would be all too easy for this tragedy to blight his life, at least they could help a little. He just hoped that whatever came up as the more permanent solution would work.

He telephoned Clare back, told her Miriam's reaction and she arranged to bring Terry round to the house at the end of the day when he returned from the library, ending the conversation by saying: "I need to do it in person, I need to check you out, you know, though Miriam tells me... you're okay." She giggled in a way that made Philip wonder what exactly Miriam had said about him.

CHAPTER THIRTEEN

You're very persuasive

Philip had been somewhat reticent about raising Mary Donaldson's situation with Miriam again. He knew it was a difficult situation and that, however reprehensible Jean Wearing's behaviour might be, it was difficult to produce absolute proof that it was criminal. Nevertheless, he wanted to do something if it was at all possible and he thought the only way to take things further was to get Miriam to actually see for herself the way the woman worked. If she agreed with him that what she did was fraudulent in any way then there would perhaps be some chance of taking things further. When he had suggested that they visit the self-styled psychic together, he was somewhat surprised that Miriam had not rejected his idea out of hand, though her initial response was a wary: "Let me think about it." So far so good thought Philip, who then found that, a little while later, it proved to be Miriam who raised the matter again.

"I think I have an idea about how we can approach that Wearing woman," she said. "I think I have a way of tempting her into declaring just how gifted she is. Not."

"Oh, okay, how exactly?" Philip replied, but Miriam just asked him to leave all the details to her. They made a few notes about each other's movements to find a time when they could both attend a meeting with the woman and Philip was pleased to find that something was going to be done, even if he did not know how far it would take them it seemed to be a first step.

"I must be mad, goodness knows what they would say at the station," she said. "But you're very persuasive and it is in a good cause, I guess."

Philip felt Terry staying with them would cause little problem, he was just pleased that he and Miriam had a plan now regarding the psychic and saw no reason to put it off because they had a guest. They were agreed. They had arranged to meet at Jane Wearing's house at lunch time today, despite the difficult nature of the morning, Miriam had not suggested cancelling it, so he assumed the visit was still on. Meantime Philip was at work in the library, blessing the fact that he was able to work flexible hours and intent on getting everything that needed to be done that morning completed before he left to meet Miriam. At the moment he was faced with a library user holding a large stack of books. The man was wearing a duffle coat and was holding a pile of books in front of him that consisted of just slightly more books than were easy to grasp securely.

"Do you have a café in here?" he asked.

"No, I'm afraid not," said Philip imagining the additional work there would be if such a thing did exist "but there are plenty nearby, I sometimes think Maldon High Street has few shops other than cafes."

"Okay, I'll find somewhere, can I take these with me for a moment?" The man, whose arms were unable to move as he clutched the stack, sort of nodded down at the books he held under his chin using his eyes to convey the problem. Philip looked at the pile wondering what on earth made the man think that was likely to be in order. "Have you never been in a library before?" he said. "Or are you a complete idiot who thinks we just give our books away in industrial quantities to anyone who wanders in? Maybe you should have brought a wheelbarrow." Of course he did not say that out loud, but instead explained with more patience than he felt that such a thing was not possible, that only so many books could be taken out at one time and that they must be registered as being withdrawn in the library system first. The man appeared about to argue, but then the pile split in the middle and the books cascaded to the floor around him. Philip tried to retain his patience and stooped to help retrieve them and at last the man departed with just two of his finds: a book about the science of black holes and a novel Philip had never even heard of which appeared to be about dragons – he appeared to be a man with eclectic tastes.

It was unsurprising, after the morning she had experienced, that Miriam was in danger of being late. She was still in two minds about her plan, but on balance felt it was a good thing to do, indeed it was growing on her and she felt the meeting might provide some light relief after the earlier difficulties. At present she was involved in yet another road accident. It seemed to her that as the volume of traffic in the area grew ever greater, the standard of driving deteriorated alongside it. It could only get worse too: like many small towns government plans to build more houses there seemed as if it could overpower it. We live in such an impatient age and so many drivers just seemed to push and push until something gave she thought. No great harm had been done in this case and no one had been injured; the main effect of the collision as one car pulled out into traffic at a junction was an argument as to whose fault it was. The young woman driving an expensive soft topped Audi was screaming at the middle aged man driving an ancient Ford Escort. He looked cowed in face of the onslaught, but was adamant that the woman's car was invisible and around the corner when he pulled out and that she must have been driving too fast.

"It is a thirty area, you know", he said, his voice a little stronger as he found a fact to quote on his side.

Her car had more scrapes than his and it was clear any claim she had to make on insurance was going to cause her grief, not least with any husband or partner there might be in the background. Meantime a significant queue of traffic had built up behind them. Miriam managed to get first the details of who was who, then the cars moved to the side of the road so that the traffic could move again. It seemed to Miriam that it was six of one and half a dozen of the other in terms of fault, though the corner was such that it did mean visibility was minimal, and she in the end she managed to pacify them and get them on their way.

Fifteen minutes later she was parked at the roadside on the other side of town, Philip drew up behind her and she joined him in his car for a moment and outlined her plan to him before they went inside. She was in uniform. Philip was amazed at what she said, it echoed one of the things he had asked on his visit to the psychic and he felt it would make an excellent test. He agreed to her suggestion without hesitation. She seemed not just to have agreed to do something, but to have entered into the spirit of the thing with gusto. She would take the lead.

"I hope she's there" said Philip, looking over at the house, "there is a car outside." A small blue hatchback sat on the drive.

"Well, let's go and see. And stick to the plan, don't say anything more than we agreed and whatever you do - don't lose your temper." Miriam gave him a hard look and added, "Promise?" Philip nodded, the last thing he wanted to do was spoil things; he turned to open the car door.

They walked up the path together, Miriam pushed the door bell and they stood waiting for a response, but they only waited for a moment. The door soon opened and Jane Wearing stood in front of them, her figure still topped by her curious hairstyle. She looked wary at the sight of Miriam's uniform.

"Good morning, Mrs Wearing, I'm Sergeant Jayne, we met a while back… when you had paint sprayed at you."

"Yes, yes, I remember," said Mrs Wearing, continuing apace, "but I did say I didn't want anything done about that. I still don't."

"Yes, that's understood, I never found out what was going on, so unless something changes I'll leave it. But it's not about that. I wonder, may we come in for a moment?"

"Well, yes, I suppose so." Mrs Wearing's expression suggested she would rather allow entrance to a rabid dog, but thought there was no alternative. Miriam had no need of her next line which would have been something along the lines of 'we can always do this down at the station', though she was well aware that in fact the circumstances wouldn't have made that possible. Jane Wearing led them into the house.

A few moments later they were sitting round the table in the room Philip had been in for his 'consultation' and Miriam explained.

"As I said, I don't want to get back into that incident. I think you know Mr Tomlinson here, as a client, he has persuaded me that you might be able to help us." Miriam remembered to use the name Philip had used when he consulted Jane Wearing.

"Err. How?" her voice was an apprehensive whisper.

"It's about a missing girl, a local teenager, do you think you might be able to help us find her, her parents are frantic. I wouldn't do this as a rule, of course, not in the course of official business, but Mr Tomlinson's an old friend and he was adamant that… well, no stone unturned I guess." Miriam was well used to speaking with authority and made every effort to make the request sound real.

Jane Wearing's expression changed from suspicious to almost eager. Afterwards Philip said he reckoned she just could not resist the opportunity to get involved, and besides saying no would have been impossible without her sounding mean and uncooperative.

"Well," she said, "I would need to know a little about her."
Miriam was ready with a potted history.

"Her name's Stacy Beck" she said, she lives in the town with her mother – she's a single parent, so common these days – she went off to school a few days ago, never got there and has not been seen since. There isn't anything suspicious about it, I mean no foul play seems indicated, but there are no clues to her whereabouts either. There was nothing in her recent behaviour to suggest some sort of problem. It's most probably just teenage angst."

Mrs Wearing nodded as the explanation continued, her eyes attentive behind her large glasses. Miriam gave her an age, a brief, and rather vague, description of the girl and added:
"I don't know much about your sort of work, but I've heard a possession can help. This is her jacket." She put the dark navy blue zipper jacket she had carried into the house onto the table saying: "Anything you can do to help us would be appreciated. Any insight, however small, might be valuable."

Jane Wearing appeared caught up in the story and made no mention of a fee for her services.

"Well I can certainly try," she said. "Bear with me a moment." She got up and took a moment to light the candles on the sideboard and then drew the curtains saying as she did so:
"This helps concentration. Bear with me… and please be quiet now."

She drew the jacket towards her and rested both hands on it, then began kneading it a little rather as a cat does with its paws as it settles to get comfortable on a blanket. She sat, her head angled down towards the jacket. Philip could not help thinking that she looked somewhat ridiculous. A long silence ensued, well it seemed like a long silence to Miriam and Philip, neither of whom could quite believe the way she had taken the story on board, though she was probably only silent for a couple of minutes. Then she looked up and spoke again:

"I can feel her presence, yes, I'm sure. And I'm convinced she is alive too, but she's upset – I can feel the emotion, she wanted time away from her mother, away from school. But I'm getting no feeling of why that was, though. Not yet."

Miriam spoke out in a soft voice, somehow the low light and the attitude of Jane Wearing seemed to call for quiet.

"It's where she is *now* that is important."

"Yes, I understand. I don't think she's far away. She's wearing something dark, a jacket, I think. She's smiling."

Well, as she had told her that the girl disappeared on the way to school, it was no great insight to envisage her wearing a school blazer, thought Miriam. Few further details were offered, although Jane Wearing could not resist keeping up the farce and offered to think about the problem some more and get in touch if she "had any further insight". Miriam thanked her and said that perhaps she could telephone in a day or two to see if anything more had come to her.

"Yes, of course. Please do," she said and found a card that she handed over so that Miriam would have her number.

After polite goodbyes all round they took their leave and returned to the cars, sitting in Philip's small Honda for a moment before continuing on their separate ways.

"Well, what do you think? Asked Philip.

"Well, she doesn't fill me with overwhelming conviction that she has second sight, about the only thing she said was that she saw my missing girl 'wearing something dark', no great revelation that, though she seemed to be certain that everything she said was confirming her gift."

"So, is there more that can be done about her do you think?"

"Sorry, I must get back to the station now, but I promise I will think about it some more and we can have a further word later on. Okay?"

Philip nodded. Miriam returned to her own car and they both continued their day. Philip drove back to the library and parked in his designated spot behind the building; he was surprised and delighted at Miriam and the action she had taken. It was, he felt, a good start, one that he hoped could go further and which might ultimately stop the wretched woman in her tracks. He couldn't wait to forget all about her. He did not realise, however, that he would in fact be crossing paths with Jane Wearing again, and doing so rather sooner than he thought.

CHAPTER FOURTEEN

Frankly nothing would make me happier.

Philip put the matter of Jane Wearing on one side, he was not due to see Mary Donaldson again for the moment and he and Miriam would not have time to discuss the matter any further for a while either. At that moment, Mac and Poy's visit was a more pressing matter; meantime his busy day continued and he forced himself to concentrate on his work. About one thing he had decided that he had total confidence. He had spent a few minutes earlier in the day talking to Margaret about her undertaking primary school visits. She had attended one reading session with him, discussed the matter with him twice and had left a few minutes earlier, clutching a folder and saying that she felt she would be okay on her first solo assignment; in fact she seemed to have moved from regarding the task as something she feared to something she quite looked forward to doing. It would be good for her to have some tasks that were her own clear responsibility and Philip believed she would now make a good job of it. The host teacher would be in touch with him from the school after the session to give him some feedback. For the moment he decided to forget about it. He had other things to do.

Besides he was confident that she would acquit herself perfectly well.

As ever, time on the floor of the library was peppered with encounters. He was asked what to do about a lost library card, and had to explain there was a charge for reissuing it; a book with teeth marks on it and mushy pages (they being inflicted by a dog) meant a charge to replace the book; and, today's gem, having taken someone over to a section containing books on astronomy he was then asked where the sub-section on fortunes for those born under the star sign Sagittarius was located. It sometimes seemed to him that there was an element of mystery about such things. On the one hand he presumed that those frequenting a library were likely to be amongst the more sensible in the population, on the other hand some questions just seemed so… well, bizarre. His colleagues told the same story, and there was always a good deal of ongoing swapping of tales about their oddest member moments amongst the small team. As he returned to and came alongside the front desk he accidentally knocked a pile of leaflets placed a little too close to the edge onto the floor. He stooped at once to retrieve them and, as he stood up again, he suddenly found himself face to face with Jane Wearing. Not what he expected, she was not to his knowledge a library user. He assumed she wanted to see him, then remembered he had given her a false name; he was not to know that she was there accompanying a friend on a trip to the High Street and had spotted him as she waited for her friend to choose a book. He had recognised her at once, of course, though she was wearing a different outfit, but her hair was still the same; so it seemed it was not an unfortunate experiment.

"Well, nice to see you again Mr Tomlinson, how are you?" she began, taking advantage of the chance encounter and spotting an opportunity to encourage him to book another session with her. Philip was taken by surprise, not just at seeing her there so soon after their meeting, but to hear her use the false name he had chosen to use on his visits to her. But what other name would she use, he thought? That was what she knew him as. For a second he was unsure how to reply.

"Oh, right... yes, I'm fine thank you," he managed, wondering what would come next. What came next followed Jane Wearing taking in the detail of the name badge everyone on the library staff always wore.

"Or is it Mr Marchington?" she queried, her expression taking on a puzzled look.

"Well yes, as you see," he paused "it is, Marchington that is." He wondered for a moment what to say, settling on:
"I'm afraid I was somewhat embarrassed about visiting you. I used another name, I suppose that was silly, but I did." He hoped his explanation sounded plausible.

"Well never mind, I can be discreet, but we were so close weren't we, shall we fix another date for you as we have happened to meet like this? You must have a diary here I'm sure." Philip had no intention of fixing another session with the woman.

"Yes, no," he was still a little flustered at seeing her again unexpectedly. "I mean I do have my diary here, but I don't want to arrange a second session." Jane Wearing's voice took on an annoying and exaggeratedly concerned tone, it made her sound as if she was speaking to a naughty small child; her demeanour had him half expecting her to stamp her foot.

"Oh surely you do. You must. We were so close, we were making good progress and I'm sure it would put your mind at rest about your sister."

"No, no more. Thank you." He aimed at projecting a firm tone and putting an end to the matter before anyone around them in the library noticed what was going on, but she demonstrated that she was made of sterner stuff; she persisted.

"But Mr Tomlinson, or can I call you Mr Marchington? It would be such a shame not to go further, I just know it would put your mind at rest, it would allow you to move on and…" Philip interrupted.

"I said no Mrs Wearing, and I really do mean no." He delivered the line his voice low but strong, intending that to be an end to the matter.

"But…" Despite his growing insistence she still made a further attempt to prolong the exchange. Philip found her persistence growing in annoyance. He resolved to put a stop to the line she was taking once and for all.

"I know it would do me no good at all. I am quite clear what my first session with you did. It demonstrated to me that you are a fraud. You prey on vulnerable people. You have no ability to talk to the dead." He was well used to dealing with the occasional difficult customer, but this felt different; he found his anger on behalf of Mary Donaldson rather getting the better of him.

"How dare you, I'm…"

"Enough. Just stop this and go." Philip found he was raising his voice. In the library. He half expected to hear himself being shushed, some of the members were great shushers. He lowered his tone, but continued.

"I am quite certain you are a fraud and I want no more to do with you. That's why I involved the police – I wanted them to know how you deceive people too and how you obtain money under false pretences. Frankly nothing would make me happier than to see you prosecuted."

"But I tried to help the police with…, I …" She stopped, perhaps now wondering if that meeting had been everything it appeared to be at the time. She found herself unsure about this now, she opened her mouth as if to say something further. It remained open for a moment, making her look somewhat fishlike, then she closed it again without further utterance. She appeared both uncertain and a bit shaken. Philip waited a moment then spoke again, offering one brief comment.

"I mean it." He spoke low but with some force. He was pleased with the impact he seemed to have had on her, but wondered if he had gone too far; Miriam was involved in this now too after all, and he wondered how this would fit with her overall plan. He had not intended to take things further and had let his feeling take matters on more than might be prudent.

Jane Wearing said no more, turned on her heel and went towards the exit. She stood there looking back and glowering at him for a few moments, then her friend, who had now checked out a book, joined her and they left the library together. Philip hoped his tone had brought her up short. His colleague who had been manning the desk alongside him during this exchange raised an eyebrow and seemed about to say something to him, but Philip anticipated him.

"Please don't ask. It's complicated, and a very long story," he said and turned and went towards his office. He would have to tell Miriam what had happened, now that his cover was blown so to speak.

An hour or so later, back at home and brooding about what she saw as Philip's apparent threat, Jane Wearing was getting over her initial shock at what had happened in the library. She went into the kitchen to make herself a cup of tea, then, having laid out a cup and saucer and as the kettle began to heat the water, she picked up the phone and punched in a number. She felt she might just need some help.

CHAPTER FIFTEEN

Trouble is exactly what you'll get

The last hour of the library's day, with closing time set at 7.00 pm, was a little different in character from other times, with most members coming in then being people at work during the day. Towards the end of what had, by any standard, been a busy day, Philip found Margaret again visiting his small office; they had earlier had a conversation about her school visit. Her reading session at the school had gone well, Philip had already received a call from the teacher at the school with whom the session had been arranged and she was well pleased with the way Margaret had handled things. Philip had found Margaret reporting back favourably too: she thought it had all gone well, she reckoned the kids would agree, the teacher had seemed pleased and, rather to her surprise, she had really rather enjoyed doing it. Not only that but she had gone on to ask if she would be able to do similar sessions again. Philip was pleased, despite her original reluctance about the task he had been sure she had potential and this had proved a good step along the way; she was an asset to the library and he resolved to let her do more. Now though she had other business and came straight to the point.

"There is a man asking for you at the desk, he won't say what it's about, but he says his name is Gary Hunt," she told him, seeming to make a point of adding, though without any explanation: "I don't like him."

"Okay, I'll come." Philip stood up, left his office and starting to make his way towards the desk. He recognised the name and wondered what it was about. His conversation with the detective had not suggested any visit was likely to follow. As Philip walked through there were still a number of people around, but no one he recognised as a regular caught his eye.

Gary Hunt was standing at the front desk, a somewhat shambolic figure with a scowl on his face that hovered somewhere between sour and threatening. He offered no greeting, but pitched right in.

"I've got a bone to pick with you," he said, pointing a jabbing figure at Philip's chest, "leave my sister alone or you'll have me to deal with, right. Understand?"

"No, not really, who's your sister?" Philip replied, not liking the turn things appeared to be taking.
"Jane Wearing. The woman you accuse of fraud."

"Okay, I have met your sister…" Philip paused contemplating a rant about the wretched woman's chicanery but, with the library going quietly about its business around them and having had one altercation so far today, he thought better of it, continuing: "I don't want any trouble here. I suggest you leave. Right now. It is not something I propose to discuss with you."

"I don't want to discuss it, I just want to say what I've said and if you don't take note then trouble is exactly what you'll get. Be warned."

Hunt put a snarl into the final words, spun on his heels and headed off towards the exit. Philip waited until he was sure he had gone, then let out a sigh and returned to his small office to find Margaret had followed him there and again stood at his elbow.

"What was that all about? I was right, I think, that's not a nice man."

Philip was about to say something by way of explanation, but Margaret continued: "Anyway it seems to be your day for unwelcome visitors," she said. "Guess what?" Philip gave her a quizzical look and opened his mouth to speak, but she was not waiting for a reply and finished with the words: "Froby's here." She pointed somewhere over her shoulder. There followed a long moment of silence when they both just looked at each other while Philip hoped he did not have to fear the worst.

Miss Frobisher, late head of the library in Maldon, was not missed in any way by her former colleagues and most certainly not by Philip who had disliked everything about how she had run the place. As her bizarre plans progressed he had worked hard in the background to make her downfall more likely, something of which he thought she had been unaware; now maybe, he thought, that had not been the case. By encouraging her hair brained schemes to turn the library into some sort of technology centre, and customer service free zone his actions had her going so far over the top that officials at the county library HQ put a stop to her inappropriate empire building. They moved her sideways, and Philip was made up to replace her. No one had ever been very sure what her motives were. She displayed no interest of any sort in books, something most would regard as a prime requirement of such a position, she had never checked out a single volume or taken a turn at the desk, and instead seemed to revel in what Philip called "admin for the sake of admin" and in her vision of a library where books were the least important of its activities. If there was a rule about something she would review it, embellish and complicate it and invent seven different cross-referenced systems to ensure its consistent enforcement. Where there was no rule she would most often want to invent one; or two. She saw those people using the library as a distraction and was certain that the smooth running of the place would be much enhanced if no one ever came in to borrow a book, and above all if they never had any queries or questions to worry staff with if they did do so. Perhaps above all she had a fixation about modernity and wanted the library to be not only a hub of white hot technology but also the envy of what she saw as its poor, inadequate and less advanced fellows in the world of libraries.

When she left, moved to a central position of some sort in Chelmsford, "hopefully in some HQ bunker" as Philip put it, he was pleased that she did seem to have been put in a backroom job and that there seemed to be no need for her to have any further contact with him and his staff. Well, apart from a string of obtuse memos sent to the heads of all the libraries in the county regarding the collection of data. Despite their length, their purpose was always almost totally unclear and ignoring them, which Philip and others around the system always did, seemed to invoke no response or retribution. The lack of any comeback seemed just to confirm their seeming purposelessness – well, until now perhaps.

Back at HQ, Miss Frobisher was also very much something of an unknown quantity. She had an office, a job title (a long one), but her job, whatever it was, seemed to demand little interaction with other members of staff and her brusque manner and obsession with rules and procedures made those around her disinclined to investigate. As one said: "She's in a world of her own and welcome to it". Another, working in a nearby office, had asked her if she would like to join his little team for lunch one day soon after her arrival. He had seen it as friendly gesture, but she had made it very clear that whatever she was doing, and she did not specify what that was, it was far too important to be put on hold for a single second. She clearly regarded a lunch break of any sort as only for the terminally uncommitted; he had remembered her unfriendly glare and had not asked her again.

Now apparently she was back. In Maldon. In what Philip now thought of as *his* library.

"What does she want?" He asked Margaret finally breaking the silence.

"No idea. She's not spoken to a soul," she replied. "She's just going round with a clipboard. I didn't think I should approach her."

It did not sound good. It did not sound good to him at all.

"Well, I better go and have a look, I suppose," he said, with a distinct lack of enthusiasm, as he left his office and went to the front desk. He did not approach Froby, who he could see away in the distance clipboard in hand, but busied himself with something at the desk merely to make it look like he had reason to be on duty there where he could see her.

Froby ignored him, and ignored everyone else too for that matter, rather she continued making a slow circuit of the public area pausing occasionally to jot down a brief note on her pad. Then, still remaining disengaged from her former colleagues, she put the clipboard she was holding into a slim leather briefcase she carried on a strap over her shoulder and headed for the exit door. Philip was appalled. He did not want whatever reason she might have for visiting the branch – his branch - hanging over him. If she was about to unleash some new piece of bumbledom on them he would be happier with some prior indication of what it might be. He had to ask. He caught up with her before she got to the exit and called out.

"Miss Frobisher." She paused, turning a little and he followed up quickly, "Hello there, is there something we can do for you?" He found he had instinctively not offer any preliminary comment such as a how are you. She stopped as she heard his voice, turned fully and looked at him over her ultra-modern spectacles, appearing a little nonplussed. Philip surmised that she had wanted to get in and out of the building unchallenged. She appeared to consider whether to reply at all, then after only a few seconds all she said was a single word:
"No."

As she stared at Philip he noticed she had new spectacle frames even more modern than the last. She added nothing, no hello, no how are you, nothing that was not essential, which was apparently just the blunt "no" she had offered. Her hair was pulled back tightly in a bun and she reminded Philip of nothing more than a skinny version of the infamous Miss Trunchbull, the severe headmistress who was the unpleasant adversary of Matilda in the classic Roald Dahl book. That brief word said she turned to go and did just that, heading left out of the door and walking off towards the car park at a brisk pace. He watched her go; she didn't look back.

Philip muttered "Rude" under his breath and then, when that seemed wholly inadequate in the circumstances he added "Bloody woman" spoken a little more loudly and made his way back to the front desk. There seemed to be no more he could do, though he concluded that any visit she made did not bode well and he resolved to be on his guard. He made a mental note to telephone his opposite number in a nearby branch to see if she had been there and if she could cast any light on the matter. Margaret looked at him inquisitively from nearby. Philip anticipated the question and said only "I have not the slightest idea what that was about, she said nothing. Well, she said 'no' when I asked if I could help. Impossible woman. I could not be gladder that she's not here anymore. I just hope that her unannounced visit doesn't mean something nasty's brewing. If any of the others ask, then just say I have no idea. We can but wait and see if her visit signifies something else to come." Margaret's face showed clear agreement, but she made no comment and returned to their earlier conversation and to his earlier visitor by asking what "the hatchet faced man demanding to see you earlier" had wanted. He had told Margaret about Mary Donaldson and Jane Wearing, indeed it was she who had started the involvement by spotting Mary crying in the corner, so Philip gave her a quick update and explained the link to Gary Hunt.

Later on, as the day concluded and his various final tasks took Philip all around the library, when he passed the notice board he could not fail to note that yet another of what he continued to think of as the "countdown cards" had appeared there. This one said THE CLOCK'S TICKING. He still had no idea about what they referred to or how they got there either, he had checked with his team again but no one had seen anyone putting one up; they, and their originator, remained a complete mystery. There had now been six of them. As Miriam had said, the purpose would doubtless become clear in due course. Meantime it was a puzzle, though one he found more and more annoying. It had begun to seem that it might only be made clear when the countdown, whatever it was, reached a conclusion. But if Miriam was right, and that was to be the end of the world, then he hoped that would be a good while ahead.

As the day's operation came to an end, and it was time to close the library, Margaret mentioned Froby again.

"Any guesses as to what she was up to coming here like that?" She asked.

"Nothing, no, I don't really know what her job is now and she seemed intent on keeping whatever it was secret. Maybe she misses us." He meant it as a joke, but it just sounded weird.

"I would love to think we will hear no more from her," he continued. But he was soon to find out that he was wrong.

CHAPTER SIXTEEN

You'd be surprised

Back home, still puzzling over what the odious Froby was doing visiting the library, and doing whatever it was she was doing without saying anything about it too, Philip had forgotten all about the time. He had been working down a list of things relating to the sale of Abigail's house, something which would occur once Mac and Poy had been through her things. He had been making good progress and wanted it to be possible for them to do most of what followed during their time in Maldon. He was now sitting at his desk at home in front of his computer sending an email to Michael and Poy about their imminent visit and the arrangements for picking them up at the airport and getting them back to Maldon. He had just clicked on 'send', when he was startled by the front doorbell ringing. He went and opened the door and found Clare Townsend, a huge multi-coloured Doctor Who-type scarf wound twice around her neck, standing on the doorstep alongside Terry, who was wearing school uniform topped with an anorak and was clutching a black zipper bag to his chest. Although he knew full well that they were coming, the fact that the time had crept up on him while he was distracted by other things, must have rather thrown him and perhaps, given Clare's first remark, his distraction showed.

"You were expecting us, weren't you?" She said, ushering Terry into the hall without ceremony and giving Philip a broad smile.

"Yes, yes of course," he replied, "I've had a bit of a day, but then you have too I'm sure," then recovering himself he added "I guess this will be my vetting, won't it? Would making you a cuppa find any favour?"

Clare gave a light laugh and nodded.

"Tea would be good. Perhaps you could show Terry where he'll be sleeping and I'll put the kettle on if that's alright. Miriam not here?"

"Nope. On duty right now, but she'll be back before Terry goes to bed. Come on in Terry… hi and welcome. I am so sorry to hear about your mother." His last remark produced an awkward silence in both of them so, after a moment, he returned to being business-like.

"You just bring your bag and follow me, although you know the layout, it's a mirror image of Abigail's'…" His voice tailed off as he realised that getting into that subject was not advisable with Clare there. The matter of Terry's unorthodox use of his "Aunt's" house was not generally known and Philip's view was that no harm had been done and that the incident was best forgotten. His remark did not seem to have worried Terry, though he looked a little subdued as he answered.

"I've not brought very many things, just enough to keep me going for a few days," he said squinting down at his bag. "There's more I really need, my computer's most important…" He paused then adding, "This is very good of you Mr M." Clare shot him a look, which Philip took to mean she was unsure about Terry calling him Mr. M, but when Philip went on as she went through to the kitchen, she said no more.

"No problem, I expect Clare will get you properly settled soon and you know you are welcome to stay here in the meantime." Terry looked unsettled, as of course well he might, and Philip added: "Anyway your place is only a little way along the road, it will be no problem to fetch anything else you need in due course. There's no problem about the computer, and we've got decent Wi-Fi here too. How are you doing?" Philip was conscious of the fate of his mother and all that flowed from it, in the face of which it was, he felt, a somewhat inadequate remark. We all find such things difficult, he thought, we end up being so careful that our comments are bland and unhelpful. Yet one had to say something. His question also appeared to be one to which it was difficult for Terry to respond. They climbed the stairs, silent again for a moment, with Philip leading the way.

"Oh, you know," said Terry ending the pause and they were both pleased to divert into a few words about bedrooms, empty drawers, cupboards and where the bathroom and the light switches were located.

"You get sorted out and come down whenever you're ready, I'll talk things through with Clare and see what she needs," Philip told him.

Back downstairs, Clare had made tea and when Philip returned the two of them sat down opposite each other at the kitchen table while Terry remained upstairs to unpack and change out of his school uniform. Clare had put the mugs of tea on coasters she had found near the kettle to protect the table.

"Now we get onto the third degree. Right?" said Philip smiling.

Clare was quick to respond: "Yes, I'll just get the thumb screws out," she said as she moved to produce a clip board from a voluminous bag made from bright flower pattern fabric, adding in a more serious tone, "There are a few questions I must ask, but it really is just a formality, I know Miriam, of course, and you are obviously a perfectly suitable household for this. I'm sure Terry will be fine. In terms of Terry's situation we can regard you as counting as a friend of the family" She clicked her pen and had the remaining details she needed noted down within a few minutes.

"There is one thing" said Philip when she appeared to be done. "You know that we both work shifts, well Miriam more than me I suppose, and so we don't keep precise nine to five hours. Terry may be alone here on occasion, is that okay?"

"No problem. He seems to be doing fine. But I'm not sure if that's because he and his mother were not that close or because her death hasn't quite sunk in yet. It always takes a while to come to terms with the facts. A bit of both I fancy. With enquiries and a post-mortem to be completed it will take a while before a funeral date is set, then there is the whole question of finding him a permanent place to live. A new home. Meantime he is insistent on continuing attending school as normal. His main worry seems to be the question of where he will be living in future. I guess that's understandable. He's worried about being moved away from his friends."

"Well, I'm sure there's a good bit to be settled, we'll keep an eye on him though – anything else?" said Philip.

"No, the rest is down to me, I'm already into the next process and should have him sorted out before too long, at least in terms of somewhere to live, so he should not have to stay with you for too long."

At that moment Terry came back downstairs and walked into the kitchen.

"All set then Terry?" said Clare "We're all done here. Room okay?"

"Yes, fine thanks" said Terry.

"Right," said Philip "I'll see you out." He addressed the last remark to Clare and then, turning to Terry added: "Just a quiet evening in for us then Terry. Miriam's left us some supper, she'll be back later."

An hour or so later, with them both well fed and with there being still no sign of Miriam returning home, Philip was wondering what on earth to talk to a fifteen year old boy about, a problem made worse because of the problems Terry had. Philip had attempted some investigation of how Terry was feeling and, though he did not say very much, it was clear that on top of the sadness about his mother, the overall feeling he had was one of uncertainty. There was so much that he did not know, with the timing of an autopsy, a funeral and the whole question of a more permanent home for him all on hold. There was an awkward few minutes about it all, and Philip ended this with an open invitation.

"I don't want to press you, Terry, I know how difficult it must all be for you but if I can help in any way, if you want to talk, ask… just say. Miriam will help too, I know. You just say."

There was silence between them again for a while, but perhaps Terry was an unusual teenager, as Philip well knew, he was a prodigious reader, and he found this gave him a lead in. They talked about what Terry was reading for a moment. This was *The Martian* written by Andy Weir. It was a bestseller.

"Good?" Philip asked, thinking it a pretty sound choice for someone moving into titles aimed at adults, though as he recalled the book had a good deal of swearing in it. Doubtless the lad heard worse at school, and besides the character was marooned millions of miles from Earth and that seemed to justify an expletive or two.

"Yeah, very, I've not seen the film yet, it will be interesting to see how it was done." There was silence between them for a moment, then Terry had a question for him.

"What's it like working in the library then?" He asked, perhaps pursuing a topic that did not relate to his own immediate circumstances and then finding it was one that Philip could talk about with ease.

Philip began with the silly things - including today's favourite: his overhearing a man sitting at one of the tables saying to another library user opposite him: "Shush, be quiet. This is a library, you know." The other man had protested: "But I didn't make a sound," he said, his face registering surprise, umbrage and uncertainty.

"No," said the other, "but you looked as if you were about to."

"You'd be surprised at what goes on. I love it." Philip told him.

Before long, as he searched for more substantial topics and considered recent events, Philip had told Terry the saga of Mary Donaldson and they were discussing various ways of parting unthinking people from their money. He soon found Terry had considerable knowledge about scams on computers. Teenagers and technology he thought, and then gave Terry the password details that would allow him to link his laptop to the Wi-Fi in the house. His own things were already connected and, like so many people, he had had to look up the right word. Not for the first time he thought about changing all of the endless list of passwords he seemed to have to a single one – maybe "IdoRemember", though a number was often demanded too. Once he had it, Terry was then able to launch into... Philip knew not what, but it was clear it needed all his concentration.

As they did this, not far away near the library itself events that would affect Philip the following morning were taking place.

✳

The car turned off the A12 and headed towards Maldon. It was no great distance from the main road to the town, but the minor roads that characterised all the small town's links with areas around it, meant it took a little while. The evening was dark when the car threaded its way across the bridge spanning the narrow channel of the river, up the steep curve of Market Hill through the town and parked near one of the town's group medical practices close to the offices of the local Council. A figure got out of the car and went into the surgery. After a few minutes the figure re-emerged and returned to the car clutching a paper bag, the receipt inside for a simple pain killer recording their visit to the pharmacy that was part of the practice. If they were asked in future about where they had been that evening the receipt would show their whereabouts.

Anyone watching might have noticed that the inconspicuous figure, dressed in a dark coat and trousers and wearing a beanie hat, did not get back into the car after putting the small package in the boot, but walked away, through the adjoining car park outside the town's Council offices, and along a narrow footpath leading towards the centre of town, where the path emerged near the back of the Iceland store and behind the High Street. The road here was a dead end, but important in giving access to one of the town's main car parks. Just a few small shops were located here, a men's hairdresser for one, and a series of passages ran from the road through to the High Street itself.

But the one significant place located here was the town library and it was to this that the figure made its way. The area was somewhat gloomy, the few lights around doing less than a complete job. Only a few people were about, and those that were there had no interest in it other than it gave quick access as they were passing from the High Street to their parked cars, hurrying in the chill evening air. No one took any notice as the figure stood outside the library appearing to scan the notices on display in the window detailing information both about the library itself and events in and around the Maldon district.

Finally, glancing round and seeing that for the moment there was not a soul in sight, the figure reached into a coat pocket and took out something in a small plastic bag. They shook it with some force for a few moments and doing so sounded a metallic rattle. Nobody heard it, or if they did they took no notice. The figure removed a canister from the bag and sprayed paint across the frontage of the library. Still no one appeared interested and, after a moment, the canister was replaced in the bag, the bag in the pocket and the figure set off again and returned the way it had come, walking back along the footpath to their parked car and driving away into the night.

Their handiwork remained. Though the spraying was somewhat imprecise and paint had dripped a little and run in streaks below some of the letters, the words "Leave her alone" were clear to see and stood out, painted in bright red letters a foot high.

✻

The following morning Philip had had no intention of walking Terry to school in any supervisory sense. As Clare had discovered, the boy was soon to be sixteen and did not need an eye kept on him as he did something he was well used to doing on a regular basis. The school was little more than a fifteen minute walk away. But they had found themselves setting out at the same time and so walked together up the High Street. Philip found he had an almost irresistible urge to keep saying "How are you?" every time he and Terry crossed paths. He would have to watch that, he knew that bland questions or comments would offer little or no help even though Terry had a lot to cope with. There was to be an inquest on his mother's body before a funeral could be arranged, and all that was still pending, Terry was in temporary accommodation and there had been no word yet from Clare about where he would go next. This morning few words were exchanged between the two of them as they walked. Philip tried "Anything special happening at school today?", but Terry was non-committal answering with a brief: "Not really." He was still adamant about attending school, but doubtless his mind was in something of a whirl.

They walked through the passage leading from the Marks & Spencer food store in the High Street towards the library, one of the town's car parks and the school beyond.

As they emerged from the passage, they saw there was a police car parked at the curb right outside the library and the reason for its presence was soon apparent as curiosity led them closer. The garish, red sprayed paint stood out for all to see on the library frontage. One of Philip's small team had arrived ahead of him and, seeing the damage, had gone inside and called the police. A constable was standing with him, notebook in hand.

"Right mess that," said Terry as they got closer, adding "I'll leave you to it." He turned right and, joining a group of four other fellow pupils walking nearby, he went on towards the car park and the school.

"Okay, I'll see you later," Philip called to the retreating figure and went to introduce himself to the policeman. After a brief look at the damage they repaired inside.

The constable sat, squeezed into Philip's small office and went through the motions, but there was not a great deal to say. Yes, it was a right mess. No the paint had not been there at closing time on the previous afternoon. No nothing like this had happened before and no he could not think of any reason for it.

"Well, what about the words?" the constable asked. "Those mean anything to you? Who's 'her'?"

Without much thought Philip had said that he could not think of any reason for the attack. But wait a minute, he thought now, as the constable posed the question and he gave the matter more consideration for a few moments, in fact of course he could think of a reason.

"There was a small incident in the library a few days back," he said and told the constable about Gary Hunt's visit and a little about Jane Wearing too; though he kept the details brief and did not mention Mary Donaldson. Miriam was involved in this too and he thought it better not to go into her role in the matter.

"So she could be 'her' I suppose. I don't think there is much more I can say, check with Miria… with Sergeant Jayne," he finished. "She knows about that, but, of course, if any of us here can do any more just say."

Of course it might have just been mindless vandalism, but given the words spelt out in paint, he felt that the likelihood was

166

that he was right about what had prompted the incident, though that did not, of course, identify the perpetrator. Apart from the obvious link to Jane Wearing and Gary Hunt there appeared to be no evidence as to which individual had done the spraying. The constable made some notes and departed promising that "it would be looked into".

He tried to put it out of his mind, he was not seeing Miriam until the end of the day and, as far as he could remember, she was in any case in Chelmsford for part of the day. She would no doubt catch up with it all soon enough. He thanked his colleague for dealing with the matter and dispatched him to Reeves, the High Street's ironmongers, to get something to clean up the paint, though he knew that could not be done at once, the constable had spoken about forensics and testing the paint before it was removed. But he did want to be ready to clean up the second they could do so; until then it would rather detract from the sort of image he felt his beloved library should have.

Besides he had work to do and then he was to collect Mac and Poy from Heathrow when they arrived on Sunday. He was looking forward to their visit and to the holiday he and Miriam would have once that was over, indeed, with flights booked, he had already been busy booking hotels. By the time he got to his desk there were already a number of notes and messages waiting to be dealt with – on top of the pile was another countdown card, the sixth, no seventh, if he remembered right; it said: TIME TO ACT.

CHAPTER SEVENTEEN

I need that

Amidst the huge, vaulted steel halls of Bangkok's international airport Michael Croft was pacing. He stopped and stood for a moment alongside one of the many large freestanding air conditioning units that kept the airport cool with less than total efficiency. Most of Suvarnabhumi airport had been built on reclaimed marsh land not so many years ago when the existing airport could no longer provide sufficient capacity, early on it had been beset by teething troubles after it opened, some of which persisted. He knew there was nothing to worry about, yet he found the whole idea of returning to England, and going back to his home town, after so long felt a little bit daunting. Until Philip and Miriam had tracked him down to tell him about his mother's death, it had been a long time since he had thought about the twenty year estrangement between them, or dwelt on it in any serious way. It had happened. It was just one of those things and the moment for putting it right had seemed long since passed; he had pushed it all to the back of his mind, not least because he knew he bore some of the blame, and ignored it. A busy life and an inherent feeling of not wanting to revisit difficult matters meant that it stayed ignored, though he sometimes wished things had been different. Certainly now he knew that it had all been unnecessary, an accident, prompted in the main by an undelivered letter, he did dwell on the years during which he and his mother could have had contact. He had no doubts about the decision he had taken to spend his life in Thailand with Poy. It was a good one. But, had things been different, his mother might have visited him, he thought, she might have accepted his purchase of his boat and his work sailing it as good decisions that gave him an attractive and successful way of life. Way back his parents had been adamant that sailing could never be a "proper job", they had wanted him to have a qualification, a career, but he had never blamed them for that, he knew that they had only wanted the best for him as they saw it and what he wanted was way outside their own experience. Considering it now he rather felt he had a career; one that included running his own, albeit small, business. Whatever she would have felt about his way of life, his certainty about one thing was total: he knew his mother would have loved Poy, who, after all, had been a prime reason for his remaining in Thailand. Always had been, still was. Just as he thought this she jolted him back into the moment.

"You okay Mac?" she asked.

"Sorry, miles away, I was thinking about England. It will be strange to be back there for a while." There was no way he would have said "back home"; he had just been away for too long. It was some twenty years since he had first visited Thailand and set up home there and during that time he and Poy had never been big on holidays, their life and work had it all - sailing the boat, beaches, warm weather, swimming - but they had travelled together for short breaks nearby in other parts of South East Asia: to Singapore, Bali, and other parts of Thailand like Chiang Rai in the north, where Poy had family; but they had never travelled further afield and had never been to England. So, a long haul flight and three weeks away was quite a big deal, both in terms of leaving their business and of visiting England.

"Different for you, many changes, strange for me, I never been there before, all new." Mac accepted that Poy had a point.

"I'm sure it will all be fine," he said, and on reflection he was sure it would.

A few days earlier he had returned to their apartment, after a day out on a sailing charter with customers, to find Poy in the bedroom with two large suitcases lying open on the bed. Both were stuffed so full that it was clear that closing them was going to be impossible; furthermore neither appeared to contain any of his clothes. He gave her a quizzical look which prompted her to a single brief comment.

"Big journey, big problem."

Poy spoke excellent English, but was still apt to do so in a clipped, rather shorthand fashion.

"And need different clothes for England... for the cold," she said.

"I thought we could buy you something here, just so that you are warm when you arrive and then buy a few more things in England. Same for me too, any winter clothes I had twenty years back are long gone. So, we'll need space in the cases to add a few extra things. By the way, you do know one of those cases is for me, don't you!"

Attempting to be diplomatic he had succeeded in persuading her to start packing again, albeit with some considerable reluctance. He had also persuaded her that England had shops; that English houses had heating, that they had washing machines too and that she did not need to pack and take every single piece of clothing she processed. Repacking took a while, a process punctuated by Poy saying "I need that" to almost everything he suggested was unnecessary and Mac trying to exert what he saw as reason at every turn; but after a while, packing done and suitcases closed, they were all ready to go. Now they waited in the transit lounge having completed their domestic flight from Phuket to Bangkok, their one suitcase each checked through to London and just a flight bag, containing warm sweaters for them both to wear on arrival to get through the current round of security checking before they were London bound. As their bags went through the x-ray machine, Philip was called back having made the machine bleep and discovered it was because he had two stray *baht* coins in his pocket. The security man insisted he walk through again and, in hyper-officious mode, also put the two coins in a plastic tray and sent them through as well, though quite why he did so was unclear. Just a bit over the top, thought Philip, remembering that it was said that the explanation for many an oddity in his adopted country was a simple "T.I.T" – This is Thailand.

"The trip will be good, for you, for me. I want to see England and you must sort out the house and all your mother's things." Poy spoke as they had emerged from separate passport

171

queues and, their passports checked, they proceeded on towards the London flight and boarded the plane.

After some twelve hours of mild discomfort punctuated by the inactivity, indifferent food and unappealing movies of a long haul flight and alleviated, Michael found, only by a good book, he nudged a dozing Poy and pointed out of the window.

"We're nearly there. That's England," he said. "We will be landing soon." Outside the plane the evening sky was darkening and lights were coming on below them on the ground. Poy looked out of the window at the patchwork of English countryside below. It did look to be rather different from home.

In England a few hours earlier, when the pair were still snoozing on board their flight, Philip had set off during the afternoon to drive round the infamous M25 and meet them at Heathrow Airport; Mac and Poy were on a flight due to arrive at 6.30 that evening. Despite the uncertainties modern traffic conditions brought to any long journey, and any long journey involving the M25 in particular, Philip had arrived at about the right time. Arranging travel on a Sunday no doubt helped. He parked the car in the cavernous multi-story car park alongside the terminal and positioned himself inside so that he could see the narrow exit used by those disembarking off flights at Terminal 3. A little while later he could see from the electronic board above him that their Bangkok flight had landed. As Mac and Poy would, he thought, have to come through separate queues at passport control, it might take a little while before they appeared. Most often nothing at Heathrow was quick. He sipped the last of a cup of tea from a cardboard container he was convinced was somehow adding the unpleasant flavour of plastic to a concoction in any case low on the appetising scale and thought of the preposterous charges just parking for a length of time long enough to pick up arriving passengers entailed. More on the positive side he thought about the trip he and Miriam would take, once their friends' three weeks in the U.K. was up and when, all being well, much of the sorting out required to clear and sell Abigail's house would by then be complete. Flight apart he looked forward to it. While he waited he checked his phone, the visitors had said they would text him when they had collected their luggage and were on the way out. There was nothing from them yet, but an email message had come in from Miriam.

Needless to say, following the paint spraying incident at the library, Miriam had soon set some investigations in train and her message summarised what had transpired since. Jane Wearing denied to the CID officer who visited her all knowledge of the incident, and claimed to have been at home alone that evening watching television. Gary Hunt also said he had nothing to do with it and had worked in his office through the evening – all alone, needless to say. The osteopath who worked on the floor below said that the light had been on upstairs as he left for the day, but of course that did not prove that Hunt was behind the door or stayed later. Neither had appeared with fingers daubed with red paint to make it easy.

Miriam's message told Philip that, in the circumstances and with no witnesses, if either of them had been involved, then a visit from the police might very well frighten them off and that she therefore felt that should be the end of the matter. In any event it seemed there was little more that could be done. Philip had the matter of cleaning the paint off the library frontage to sort out, and this could, he assumed, be done now inquiries seemed to have been concluded. It seemed to him that Gary Hunt's attitude when he had visited the library was indicative of his being involved, though he could, of course, have had someone else do the spraying deed itself. Never mind, he hoped that would be an end to the matter; he had other things on his mind. He sent a thank you to Miriam for the message without further comment.

Just a couple of minutes later Philip's mobile phone beeped again. This time it was the text that he expected. In two brief words it said "Coming through" and, as he slipped the phone back in his pocket he spotted the pair of them wheeling their luggage out into what the airport authorities referred to as the greeting area; this was in fact a chaotic and too small area in which moving people struggled to get past those who had stopped dead in the middle of the walking area to try and locate whoever was meeting them. He waved, was spotted in turn and they kept moving and came over. Philip shook Mac's hand, gave Poy a hug and a kiss on the cheek and greeted them with a cheery "Welcome to England." Poy's reply did not surprise him. She wrapped her arms around herself as she said: "Gee, it cold!" Mac laughed.

"I've heard her say that a few times already and we're not out of the airport yet," he said. "What's more I reckon we may be hearing it some more over the coming days." Truth to tell he was chilly himself; it was a long time since he had been in England and he felt winter temperatures might take some getting used to after living for so long in a hot climate.

"Let's get to the car then" said Philip. "The heater will soon warm you up. Then I'll get you to Abigail's house. Miriam has it all set up for your stay."

After negotiating a series of roundabouts to get back onto the M25, the bland motorway journey was not much of an introduction to England for Poy or a clear update of how things had changed since Mac was there last. After a little more than an hour Philip turned the car onto the A 12 and headed north. Again there was not much to see, but Philip pointed out to Poy that they were now heading away from London and that much around them was countryside. While Mac knew the town, he had never been to his Mother's last home in Maldon and Philip spent a little time describing it and its location to him as they went along.

Back in Maldon, Philip could have just given Mac the keys to Abigail's house, but he wanted to show him in in person and he felt also that, at some stage, he must tell him that what was now his house had had an intruder in it a little while back. No real harm had been done in his view, but nevertheless it should he felt be mentioned. With Terry staying with himself and Miriam, Mac and Poy would be bound to meet him so he did not want any awkwardness to occur. They had all met without problem in the airport terminal, though in its usual way Heathrow had added difficulty to a long flight: the plane had arrived on time, but then circled for forty minutes before landing. Now in Maldon, albeit tired from the long journey, they were all set to stay in Abigail's house; Miriam had insisted on making up the bed and making sure the house was "suitably warm" as she put it, adding to Philip, "remember they live in a hot country." He put the key in the lock and led the way into the hall, Mac and Poy following him and between them they brought the luggage inside. Even now as he entered the house again Philip half expected to find Abigail sitting in her favourite chair in the living room, ready to make him a cup of tea – or rather to let him make one for both of them as she used to do – and to discuss and swap her library books, which Philip used to ferry to and fro for her. She had been a lovely lady and he still missed his chats with her. But of course tonight the house felt empty.

"It's a pity you are seeing it like this," said Philip "Abigail had a warm and welcoming home here."

"I can sort of see that." Mac stood quiet looking around and taking in his surroundings for a moment, before Poy piped up.

"It's cold now," she said with feeling. Despite Miriam's attention to the heating, she continued a constant refrain expressed ever since she had arrived in England on what was her first trip away from the perpetual heat of South East Asia, her feeling made worse no doubt by walking into the empty, already neglected feeling, house. She wore a thick pullover, which they had purchased before they left Thailand in anticipation of the change in temperature. Despite its shapelessness she still made it look as if it was one of the most stylish outfits she possessed. This belayed the fact that the colour clashed somewhat with the warm corduroy trousers she wore – she had trouble pronouncing the word corduroy, which seemed to contain the Thai word *aroy,* meaning delicious and applied most often to food – *delicious trousers?*

"Okay, I'll turn the heating up a bit and show you how the boiler works" Philip told Mac. "You're going to spend some time here sorting things out after all so you need to be comfortable. Okay Mac? Remember the bills come to you from now on."

"Fine, turn it up, we'll pay." said Mac, glancing at Poy for approval and following Philip through into the kitchen, leaving her in the living room. She took in her surroundings, trying to imagine the room as the hub of Abigail's home, then wandered through to the kitchen and, finding the two men busy going through the boiler controls, she set off and did a little tour of the house.

"Very nice house," she said, coming downstairs again and aiming her remark through the kitchen door at Mac's back. "Make our apartment seem very small."

Mac said nothing, feigning still giving attention to the boiler, but he knew he was on the slippery slope; in due course as night followed day, once money from the sale of this house was available, they were going to move. He was not a worrier by nature and did not propose to get upset about it, or about the trip for that matter, it needed to be done, he was sure he would enjoy the visit, they got on well with Philip and Miriam and they had been so helpful. Everything would be sorted. He doubted that he and Poy would ever have got on so well if he had been a worrier: the Thais had a saying that *farang,* their term for Western foreigners, carried their worries with them like a dog does fleas. Besides he did need to think about what to do with his inheritance.

They toured the house together looking in each room. The bed was made up for them in what had been Abigail's room. It was now getting on for ten o'clock and both the visitors were tired after many hours of travel and a move to another time zone. Philip reckoned there was no more to be done that evening.

"Okay, I'll leave you to it, you know where everything is, there's some basic bits and pieces in the fridge if you want a snack. You get a good night's sleep and we can meet up in the morning. I am in the library for the first hour or so tomorrow, but Miriam will be home. No hurry, call us, knock on our door, whatever, we can have breakfast – or lunch if it's later - and go on from there."

✫

Back home Philip told Miriam their friends were all settled in and they spent a few minutes talking about the week to come as Terry sat with headphones clamped to his head and with his laptop on his knee. He seemed content with present events, though he still refused to say more than a word or two about his feelings about his mother's death; his main concern still appeared to be apprehension about the future.

As they sat there was a sudden thump by the front door.

"What's that?" asked Miriam, "someone at the door?"

"Not sure," said Philip, getting up and going into the hall to check it out. Terry, eyes fixed on his screen, didn't move, the level of disturbance necessary to rouse any teenager from computer activity well demonstrated as being higher than the thump that had just occurred. Philip stood for a moment in the hall, but there was no repetition of the noise. He opened the front door. No one was nearby. Then he noticed that here was a chip was out of the wall alongside the front door and a brick was laying on the doorstep. It appeared to have been thrown at the house. He went forward to the gate and looked each way along the road, but nothing showed as in any way connected with the incident. No one was visible who appeared to be hurrying away. The street was quiet. He returned inside.

"Someone just chucked a brick at us," he told Miriam. "Good luck: it hit the brickwork so the door and windows are okay, a vandal with an inaccurate aim, I guess." He finished by making light of it, but did, in fact, worry as to what was going on.

"In all likelihood it was the same person as trashed the library," offered Miriam, "I wonder what's going on. I thought that would stop. If it is connected to our psychic friend then we may need to check things out some more."

"Let's not worry about it for the moment" said Philip "I won't dial 999 and we'll just see what happens. We've other things to do at present, haven't we?" he looked across the room at Terry. He remained oblivious and absorbed in what he was doing. Nevertheless Philip wondered if he should be warned, so as they finished up and all made to go to bed, Philip told him what had happened, linking it to what Terry had witnessed on the way to school the other day.

"I don't know what you are up to on that computer of yours," he finished, "but when you are on that you don't notice anything. Just be aware and keep your eyes skinned in case anything else happens."

"Is it that Gary thingy?" Terry responded, "I can't remember his name."

"Hunt. Gary Hunt. We can't be sure, but he does seem a likely suspect. Him or someone he's put up to it. Don't worry about it, come on now – bed. Monday tomorrow, back to school."

Terry shut his laptop and followed Philip towards the bedrooms. He didn't propose to worry, but he did make a mental note of the name.

CHAPTER EIGHTEEN

Something he missed

Poy had negotiated Mac's two week visit suggestion to three and she was right, and it soon became apparent that they would need all of that time to do justice to both the task and the visit. First they had to get things in Abigail's house sorted. They pitched in, at first doing so with very little system. But various cupboards and drawers were opened; their contents inspected, categorised and sent in various directions. Some black bags made their way to the Farleigh Hospice charity shop in the nearby High Street, others to the rubbish. It was a start. And secondly other things were done too.

"We take time to be tourist now." Poy insisted she wanted to see a little of England and, on reflection, Mac discovered that he wanted to visit his old haunts along the River Blackwater where he had spent so much time in his youth. The two of them had a trip to London, "must see Buckingham Palace," said Poy then listing a variety of places that for her characterised England's capital. They got the train from the station in nearby Witham, they visited some of the traditional sights, booked into a budget hotel while Mac expressed incredulity at how prices in the U.K. had gone up, though it was pointed out to him that as more than twenty years had gone by it was not surprising that there had been changes. They went around central London on an open top tourist bus, they visited Poy's top must see, Buckingham Palace, where Poy declared it "rather small" and Mac did have to concede that Bangkok's opulent Grand Palace did make the Queen's London home look a little pedestrian. While peering through the railings, Poy acknowledged that it was "nice England has Royal family too", a remark being explained by the fact that the King is regarded as so very important back home in Thailand.

They visited The Tower of London, which Poy acknowledged was much grander than Buckingham Palace; she spoke to one of the colourfully dressed traditional Beefeaters who told her the story of how it is believed that if the ravens ever dessert the Tower, then disaster would follow. He stated all this with great seriousness prompting Poy to turn to Mac and say:

"And you reckon us Thais are superstitious!"

They returned to their bus ride, ending up eating a meal at a restaurant in Covent Garden after wandering around the market stalls there and watching one of the street entertainers perform with an absurdly high mono-cycle. Their early meal over, they were off to the theatre. Philip and Michael had conferred about this and had picked a perennial hit: the musical "Cats". Philip had thought of Siamese cats as he had suggested it, he just didn't know what sort of thing they'd like, especially Poy. When they arrived they had talked about it a bit.

"Siamese cats come from Burma," Poy had explained. "But Thai people like cats, like beautiful blue grey Korat cats best, but pets are for rich people. Many temples have cats, many cats, monks take care. Feed them. You have cat in Thailand you not want, you take to temple; cats eat rats and mice too. Everyone happy." After that an elaborate discussion about T.S Elliot's poems had seemed unsuitable. They both enjoyed the show.

After a night spent in their budget hotel they went to the Thames embankment and then caught a high-speed boat to travel down the river, speeding passed all the recent development in Canary Wharf and the East End, none of which Mac had seen, to Greenwich where they did a tour of the famous ship *Cutty Sark*. Poy was fascinated by the ship but, despite a bright day and a borrowed coat said she felt "a bit cold" and Mac found a good many changes in, well pretty much everything, perhaps most the volume of traffic, the crowds and the number of languages they heard spoken around them in the city, which was busy with tourists even though it was winter. It was something of a whistle-stop tour, but they both enjoyed it. On the train back to Essex they talked about what else remained to do with the house.

The following day back in Maldon there was more to do before returning to the clearing up: they went with Philip and Miriam to the car park at Heybridge Basin, left the car and walked to where the canal – the official name of which was "The Navigation" – ended in a lock where it met and joined the river. The tide was in and they crossed the narrow pedestrian bridge formed on top of the lock gates going over the canal and on the other side they walked along the footpath towards Maldon.

"This is where my parents kept a boat," Michael had said as they first arrived alongside the canal. They had started by walking a little way along the waterway towards the lock, where boats of various sizes were moored on either side of the channel, once a route to London taken by boats transporting hay for horse drawn vehicles in the city. At some moorings were small sailing boats, some motor launches, but there were house boats too, people lived there. Mac had then directed them across the lock and they walked on alongside the river, with much here being just as he remembered it.

"This is where I learnt to sail and grew to love it," he said pointing out across the river, which was a wide expanse because of the high tide and ran ahead of them towards a ninety degree turn into Maldon in the direction they were walking and alongside Northey Island in the other, where the channel turned and aimed towards the sea a few miles further on. With the tide high a wide expanse of water was created along seven or eight miles of estuary, one on which Philip had loved sailing.

"In those days this seemed a huge area to sail in, then when I moved from here to sailing from Singapore to Phuket, I spent several days going across open sea, well, ocean I guess, a bit different, eh?" He referred to the job he had got years before assisting with moving a boat to the island he now called home.

"Here great place for boats, but cold, water must be like ice. I never see ice except in fridge," said Poy with a shiver, "our sea at home much better."

"It's only really cold in the winter" said Mac "believe it or not, in the sailing season people do swim here, though I grant you it is not quite like Thailand!" Poy gave an exaggerated shiver at the very thought of people going voluntarily into the water. After a while they turned and walked back and having climbed back across the canal, at the lock connecting it to the river, they had lunch in one of the pubs and sat looking out across the river. Mac drank a pint of English beer and admitted that it was something he now found he had missed. Poy took a sip and returned at once to her lager without saying a word. Her face said it all. She ate sausage and mash, following Mac's description of it as a 'traditional English dish' she should try, without comment too, but seemed content to have seen something of where Mac's love of sailing had begun. They talked with Philip and Miriam about their coming trip to Thailand.

"You must sail with us again," said Poy, and Miriam could immediately imagine the warm sea and sunshine of Phuket.

"Not long now," she said.

After one of those moments which sometimes happen when a group of people are chatting and everyone stops talking at once, Miriam changed the subject and posed the question: "I wonder how Terry's getting on?" Caught up in their preparations for their departure to Thailand his situation had been rather overlooked. He had almost at once got into a routine with them, and his staying for a while had presented no problem. Claire had been in touch several times and it seemed that the prospect of Terry getting a permanent formal placement and moving in with a proper foster family was getting closer, though she had refused to be drawn on exactly what might be in prospect, saying that she didn't want to give false hope and that such things often took time.

"Oh, I'm sorry," said Philip "I meant to mention I had a text from him this morning, I would guess he sent it as he walked to

school, he didn't say much, let me read it." He pulled out his phone and a couple of clicks later read a single sentence:
`visiting poss foster fam after school clare will c me back 2 urs l8r` ☺

"The language and punctuation leave something to be desired, but it ends with a smiley face, so I think we can take it that a good start has been made. Clare is very professional and you can see Terry trusts her. Maybe he's going to see what will be his new home, but it must all be a bit daunting to say the least. I've told him he can keep in touch with us, with Abigail gone, we should perhaps substitute and keep a bit of an eye on him. For the moment let's just enjoy the meal." He changed the subject, returning to their visit to Heybridge.

"I have to say that being here brings back a great many memories, though I don't think I could have built a sailing business here if I had stayed."

"Big disaster if you stayed – you not meet me!" said Poy making everyone laugh.

"That deserves a toast," said Miriam raising her glass. "Here's to boats and significant meetings. You do realise that without your disappearance, Mac, Philip and I would probably never have got together."

"I'll drink to that," said Philip, "and it was around here I got the first clues that helped me track you down, Mac, the boatyard you did some carpentry work for is still there." He pointed out of the pub window in the general direction of the river and thought back, remembering how stubborn he had been; the quest to find Michael had turned into something of an obsession and it had not only been successful, but had also led to such a change in his life. As the meal ended it was Mac who adopted a practical tone.

"This has been a nice interlude, but I guess we should get back to the house, I think, there's still a good deal to do."

They walked back to the car and returned to clearing up the house.

CHAPTER NINETEEN

A meaningful memento

The following day, with the tourist part of the trip concluded for the moment, Philip had taken some leave to give a hand to Mac and Poy as the continued to clear matters up at Abigail's house. By mid-morning, after spending a while wandering at random from place to thing and on to other things, they were contemplating the job that remained to be done.

"I'm not sure I know what to do next," said Mac after a while as they sat down at the kitchen table with cups of tea.

To give them a moment Philip broached the subject of the intruder, though he now found it hard to think of Terry in quite that light. It did not prove too difficult, Mac listened and declared that he saw it as no problem, it was an incident now in the past – *mai pen rai* as the Thais say (meaning "never mind" – or rather a very broad and all-embracing version of never mind). He did express interest in what the situation was with Terry now he was left alone, and when he heard about the fact that his mother had been a kind of proxy aunt to him and had known the family. Both Mac and Poy had heard snippets about Terry at Philip's house, and met him too, though they had not spent long together, and they knew that his situation still needed a good deal of sorting out.

While they had discussed this Poy had been devising a plan. They had already done a fair amount, albeit on a rather ad hoc basis. Now it was time to ensure that the house was ready for sale; indeed doing so was the prime reason for their visit. There was nothing there of any great value, no priceless paintings or ancient Ming vases; Abigail had had something of a thinning out of her possessions when she downsized and moved house after her husband died.

"Not so difficult," she pronounced. "We cannot use furniture, too far to send, so we should move that first, if Philip and Miriam not want we should sell, how we do that?" She looked at Philip as she spoke.

"Yes, some things may be saleable, I can fix that," he said "and with that done it will give more space to sort everything else, perhaps we should keep the table to work on. I'll ask Miriam, you know she's on duty at the moment, to come and look in case there is anything she would like us to keep. I would very much like to find something, furniture or otherwise, to keep as a memento of Abigail."

Poy then went through several other suggestions.

"Clothes no good for me or Miriam, cannot sell, give to charity. Okay?"

"Fine," Mac nodded and Philip chipped in saying he would take them to "his favourite local charity", Farleigh Hospice, one of whose shops was in the town's High Street, and where he had already taken some stuff as they first began the clear up. They both knew about the death of Philip's first wife and agreed at once that that sort of decision should be his. Also agreed without argument was that books were to be for Philip to sort and look after too. He might keep some and donate others to the Library. Item by item they went down the list, Poy to the front of the conversation displaying a very practical turn of mind about it all, but also great sensitivity: she suggested that she rather than Mac take clothes to the charity shop because "easier for me, I not know Abigail." They discussed hiring a small skip (some things would need to be thrown away) and maybe a van, perhaps for a day (some things might need to be moved). Philip had the local knowledge, but would have to leave the work in the house to the other two as he was working during most of the week. They could all meet up and consult in the evenings, sessions to come that Poy would dub "peaceful councils of war".

They were joined mid-afternoon by the estate agent, a young woman who was called Melanie and looked nothing like the shark-like image of the typical estate agent. Philip had got two agents round, this one had seemed to be the most professional, had made the highest valuation and Mac had said he was happy to go with Philip's choice. Melanie had prepared a fact sheet about the house and they agreed a date for it to be put on the market; Mac signed the contract with her. She then raised the question of decoration. It had been a while since Abigail had had any painting done; Melanie's advice was that some key areas in the house should be given a once over in a colour she described as "something neutral". She was confident that a sale would be easier and the price the house commanded higher with this done.

"It won't just pay for itself, it will make you extra money," she said, directing her comment at Mac.

"I'm not sure about that, won't it delay matters?" Mac sounded sceptical. "We have a return flight set."

"The house won't be sold before that anyway," suggested Philip "I can pop in from time to time to see any decorating is all being done okay. I thought this might be the case, I've checked out decorators and have a firm in mind. I'll call the guy now and we can get an estimate." Melanie nodded approval.

"I think that's me done for the moment, I'll leave you to it," she declared and took her leave. All that was necessary now was to let her know a confirmed start date for the sales process. After she had gone Philip raised another issue.

"We also need to set up solicitors for you and see how the house purchase, when it happens, can be signed off when you are back overseas. I have a meeting fixed for you with a firm I have used myself." Again Philip had already done the ground work and he added "I've made an appointment for you tomorrow afternoon. The office is at the top of the High Street, I'll give you the details."

"Okay, it sounds like everything necessary can be set up in the next little while, and you will have a watching brief over the last stages Philip. Are you sure that's okay? I know you promised to help my mother but we seem to be loading a good many things on you. Are you sure it's not too much?"

"It's a fair swap," said Philip, "what you are doing for me is kind of important too." Mac and Poy both grinned. The holiday Philip and Miriam now planned and their returning to Thailand all together had already been discussed. Philip was in charge of the details and wanted where they would stay to be a surprise for Miriam.

Over the next week or so much of the sorting out was completed as Mac and Poy continued to work with gusto. Arrangements were made with the solicitor and the decorator who Philip had in mind contacted and briefed about the house; the work would start once Philip and Miriam were back in England after their holiday. It was all inside work, just what the decorator wanted in the winter months. But, with much of the sorting out done, one thing rankled with Mac.

You know," he said, "It's a shame, but nothing in the house holds real memories for me, my time in England was too far back and, after all, this was not the actual family home I was brought up in. I'd have liked to keep something special."

Until the unfortunate loss of contact with his mother, he had enjoyed an ordered and happy childhood, his parents were wholly supportive and family relationships were good. He looked back and considered that he had been lucky with his upbringing. He felt it would have been nice if there had been a meaningful memento of some sort, something he would value and want to retain. Philip had laid claim to a small, glass fronted bookcase on the basis not only that it was a nice piece of furniture, but also because, as far as he was concerned, no one could have too many book shelves. He could put that to good use and knew it would always remind him of Abigail. Then towards the end of the clear up, Mac was in the living room sorting through paperwork when Poy called to him from upstairs. He went up the stairs and found her standing on the small landing.

"What there?" She pointed upwards as she spoke indicating a hatch in the landing ceiling that seemed likely to provide access to a loft. No one had thought of that. Mac brought a chair from one of the bedrooms and, placing it beneath the entry, climbed up and opened the hatch to disclose a pull-down metal ladder; he extended it down. No doubt unused for many years, it squeaked a bit, but it still worked fine. Up he went, torch in hand (they had found one in the kitchen) and discovered there was a light inside. He clicked it on. The bulb was low voltage, but was sufficient to show that the loft was dusty and did not appear to have been used in any way for many years, perhaps ever since Abigail moved into the house.

"Not much here," he said "just an old trunk. I better bring it down."

It was a traditional looking, old style ribbed trunk; it was the sort of thing pupils in the Harry Potter stories had taken on the train as they had travelled to begin a new term at Hogwarts. With some difficulty Mac lowered it down, Philip receiving it and sliding it to the floor. They put it in the living room, an area now devoid of most of the furniture, found it unlocked and opened it up.

"Well, I'll be ..." Mac was dumfounded. It was full of his sailing paraphernalia from the family boat he sailed as a child and later just before he went overseas. The family boat "Starcounter" was named because of his father's love of the clear night skies you saw sometimes when moored in some quiet secluded spot overnight, one with little distracting light around to detract from the starry spectacle above.

Poy watched his face and told him "Okay, maybe now you have something for memory."

He did too. They went through the contents one item at a time. Some of what they found was now useless of course; canvass items had begun to deteriorate. But there were a number of things he would keep and treasure: the most important was an old brass compass housed in a beautifully turned polished walnut box. His father, who had always encouraged his passion for sailing until he had wanted to make a career of it, had given it to him for a birthday present as a teenager. He remembered regarding it as the best such gift he had ever received and he could imagine it already in pride of place on board his current boat. Modern navigation aids were all very well, maybe even essential, but this would make a real statement. He smiled as he rubbed the box with his sleeve, pleased to see the polished wood still appeared fresh and unmarked.

They told Philip and Miriam about the find in the evening over supper. They were sitting together in the Thai restaurant at the top of the High Street, one in which Philip and Miriam had spent a first evening out together. They talked about Abigail and reviewed the progress of the clear up job. Not only did Poy still notice the cold, which she proclaimed "like arctic" despite vigorous action on the thermostat, but she had also been missing what she called "proper food"; she pronounced it pretty good here too even if she had to be persuaded not to make an ad hoc inspection of the kitchen.

"I'm pleased you've found something to keep and remind you of old times," Miriam told Mac, "and you know what this means don't you?"

"What?" Mac asked, though he guessed what she would say and could not quite bring himself to say it himself.

"Your mother never gave up on you, or she would never have kept such things, she always hoped you were going to come home. It was such a shame you lost touch – and all because a letter went astray – but you must never think she didn't care. She obviously did."

"She even used a private detective to try and find you," said Philip and explained how he had not only found the business card in the house, but also come across the man later. He explained the circumstances, linking it to his tale about the self-styled psychic. He ended:

"Miriam's right, she never gave up on you, even though that detective was pretty ineffectual, I think, anyway I am sure you have done her proud since."

There was a silence round the table. Mac just nodded, it had made him think and his face betrayed his being affected by the thought. Poy put her hand on his as Miriam thought that it was a great shame that Abigail never knew what a successful and happy life he had made for himself, albeit far away from home.

After a few moments, Philip felt it was time to change the mood and the topic.

"I won a bet today. In the library. Remember my erstwhile boss, that wretched Froby woman?" He used the name by which the officious Miss Frobisher had been called behind her back. They all nodded, they had heard his tales.

"Well I bet one of my colleagues that I could accumulate a two inch pile of her memos from headquarters without replying to any of them before she started chasing me for a reply to her bureaucratic nonsense. Today we had an official measuring and I was declared the winner. I don't know what that woman does, she sends out an endless stream of notes and requests for information yet there is no clue as to what it's all for. As most of the branch libraries ignore her missives and their doing so causes no reaction, they are likely to be of no real substance. Admin for the sake of admin." He sighed and smiled; he was so grateful she was gone, though he did not mention her recent sudden unexplained visit. He still worried about that, thinking that maybe she was not yet out of his life for ever.

Restaurant meal over the visitors went back with Philip and Miriam for a cuppa before the evening ended and they returned to Abigail's house to sleep; even now they were still suffering a little from the long journey and the time change.

CHAPTER TWENTY

It will do the job

At a house on the outskirts of Maldon, in a road near the football club and a local favourite the Izumi Chinese buffet restaurant, it was evident that Kate Bull was not having a good day. She sat at the large scrubbed pine kitchen table ignoring the cake making paraphernalia spread about around her with a handkerchief held up to her face. She was not sobbing, but her quiet snuffling clearly indicated a problem. A flower pattern mug of tea stood ignored and getting cold at her elbow. She was missing Jack. He was alive and well, but she was not the first woman to react with sadness to what had become known in recent years as empty nest syndrome. She was managing fine, but when the post came that morning, while her husband William was out at work, there was a card from Jack amongst the routine dross of circulars and bills. He had joined the army and was now stationed in Germany, not so far away, but then not at home either. At least he was keeping in touch.

She told herself not to worry, but she did: he was all grown up now, after all, but he was also far away, he was in the army, training to kill people for goodness sake, in a situation where being in dangerous situations might be the norm and… she tried to pull herself together. He was training to be an engineer, it was a great career, he was happy - according to the note she had opened this morning at any rate, and she had no reason to doubt it. It was no real surprise, it had been his ambition for a while, he was convinced it was the right move and it looked like he was being proved correct. But it was receiving that card which had somehow made her sad despite its upbeat content.

She stood up, stuffed the handkerchief away, gave up on the tea, tipping the cold mugful down the sink and switching on the kettle to start again as she returned to her cake making.

"This can't go on," she found she spoke the phrase out loud to the empty kitchen, in her mind she made a firm resolution: when William came home they would talk about it. Meantime she finished preparing her cake mix and put it in the oven. Rinsing her hands afterwards she went through to the living room: she had a telephone call to make.

✣

Clare Townsend was busy as ever. Her job always involved juggling a number of priorities, most often with some emotional overtone and always with a degree of urgency. The department was understaffed, George was on long term sick leave, budgets were being cut – again - and to say things were hectic was a huge understatement. Nevertheless she enjoyed her work and sometimes she felt she could make a real positive difference to peoples' lives even if it took a battle to extricate a good result from the difficult situations and seemingly endless form filling involved. Sometimes though, circumstances, which so often conspired to make things slower, more complicated and difficult, could work the other way: sometimes, just sometimes, there were positive coincidences that helped reduce the battles a little.

First thing this morning she had reviewed her to do list, ever growing to do list it seemed, and was already busy on a number of different fronts. All cases were important, of course, but one case she did find herself giving particular priority to at present was that of Terry Walsh. In part this was because he had lost his mother in a horrible way and had already spent time struggling without her even before he knew what had happened to her. But it was also because the way his case had come up involved the police sergeant Miriam Jayne who she not only knew, but who was now also involved with Philip the library, as she thought of him, in looking after the boy on a temporary basis. She reflected on the fact that some people just seemed to have a natural tendency to help others. Just as well, she thought, otherwise her job would be even more difficult than it was. Her musing was interrupted by a colleague, sitting a little way away across the large, open plan office, a space that made the much hyped phrase "the paperless office" seem like a myth of epic proportions. Every desk seemed to be groaning under the load of files, papers and other workplace detritus. It seemed that time for a tidy up never got onto anyone's to do list.

"Are you coming to the HR meeting this morning?" Mary spoke loud enough for her voice to travel across the room.

"I suppose I should, yes" replied Clare, who had some vague memory of a memo, and thinking that the very last thing she wanted to do was sit in a terminally boring meeting discussing changes to some obscure procedure.

"Well, the meeting room's been changed, it's in M 8 now, see you at 11.00."

Clare grunted an acknowledgement, resolving to find something else more important to do and found her mind returning to Terry Walsh. She had met Terry a couple of times since their first meeting at his school. He remained adamant that he should continue to attend his classes, indeed it was her view that, if he could cope with this, it would be good both for his mental state and for his education; it would not be long before he had exams looming. Nevertheless he had lost his mother and despite the fact that they appeared not to have been all that close, at least in a practical sense, the emotional shock and subsequent grief was not to be underestimated. There was doubtless love there too. Being brought up by a single parent, and without any other close relatives as far as she could detect, he had no obvious adult person to talk to about the matter. She had made a note on his file to talk to him about grief counselling, some such schemes were available directed at children, for instance from the local hospice. She had put various inquiries in train regarding his circumstances, but it seemed that his father, who had left the family many years ago, was untraceable. Even if he could be found it was Clare's experience that locating him might help little or not at all. He had had ample opportunity to be involved in his son's life if he had wanted to be and there had never, according to Terry, been any contact at all since he had walked out. He might be anywhere and living under any name. She well knew that the only long term solution was to get Terry into a permanent home. It might be difficult to do, it might take some time; most foster parents wanted younger children, tended to make negative assumptions and viewed what some thought of as 'stroppy teenagers' as coming with a 'potential problem' label attached.

Terry meantime was gradually coming to terms with how things now were in his life. The situation was, well it was what it was. He knew it could not be reversed, all he wanted was an end to the uncertainty, to know where and how he would now live. He liked Clare Townsend, and had some confidence in her being able to help him, but he knew that circumstances played a large part. He could only go somewhere that was available, to a family that decided that they wanted him, and that might be anywhere at all.

The previous evening he had arranged to go home with Jackson after school, both to have a meal with him and his parents, but also to work there on their homework.

"How are you doing J?" he asked as they sat on opposite sides of the table in the dining room both writing a history essay. They had conferred a little as they worked and Jackson's father had come into the room to turn the volume of the music accompanying their work down – twice.

"Okay, nearly done," his friend replied. "Do you want a drink?" When Terry agreed Jackson went through to the kitchen and returned with two cans. On his return Terry had his computer switched on.

"Thanks. What do you think about this?" he indicated the screen and Jackson pulled up a chair beside him.

"When they said we should do a computer project, I don't think they had this sort of thing in mind. It's not what we talked about, so why this, what's it for?" Terry explained in some detail and very soon had a collaborator. After a while they had advanced Terry's original idea to a significant degree.

"That's great," said Terry reviewing their progress, "it will do the job."

"It will indeed, if you're sure about it," said Jackson. "But you do know it's still not suitable for the school project."

Clare was ready for a break. She had been hard at work for an hour or so without her accustomed morning cuppa. She stood up, stretched, but she had taken a mere step or two towards the department's coffee machine when the phone on her desk rang. She sat down again and picked it up; so much for taking a quick break.

"Clare Townsend, hello," she said. There was the briefest hesitation at the other end, a hesitation that Clare was used to – so many of the conversations that she was involved in seemed to be difficult. It was a woman who then spoke.

"It's Kate, Kate Bull, Clare, I don't know if you remember…" Again a brief hesitation, but Clare well remembered her. She prided herself on keeping in touch with those she helped.

"Of course I remember," she said. "How are you, and have you heard from that lad of yours?" She also remembered Jack leaving to go into the army and his subsequent posting to Germany.

"Yes, I'm fine and yes, I got a card from Jack this morning. He seems well. He's still in Germany and seems to be enjoying it though I get the impression that some of the training is pretty tough."

"I'm sure it is, but if he's enjoying it that's the main thing and he'll get a good technical qualification too if he sticks with it. Now, what can I do for you?"

"I wondered if we could meet…" again a slight hesitation "I could come to your office, I don't want to take up your time, I'm sure you are as busy as ever."

"Well, it would certainly be good to see you, you are one of our stars you know, a number of kids well looked after over many years. But what's it about?"

"It's, well, I miss Jack. I suppose I sort of have withdrawal symptoms. If William and I are not too old now I wondered if…"

"You'd like a new lad to foster?" Clare chipped in, she didn't wait for elaboration, but continued, "you may just have called at a time when that could help me no end. I have to be in Maldon later this morning, if I call in about midday can you put the kettle on and we can have a chat?"

They confirmed a firm meeting and Clare sat back elated, it was always a joy when those who did a great job as foster parents, returned for more. She headed for the coffee machine feeling that a break was now well-deserved.

"You look like the cat that got the cream," said one of her colleagues sitting nearby as she went by.

"You might just be right," she said "fingers crossed". She smiled to herself as she poured the mug of coffee she just had time for before she left and thought what a shame is was that she would now miss the H.R. meeting; she did not feel even the slightest pang of guilt.

Just before midday Clare pulled her car into the Bull's driveway. Back at her offices an H.R. meeting was under way. From the memo advising her to attend she knew that the introduction promised a "consultative and interactive session" at which "proactive action" would be suggested using a "new matrix-based approach" to, well Clare was not very sure what it was all aimed at. She had emailed her apologies, pleading that she had a "possible breakthrough" on a difficult case to which she must attend. Maybe, she thought, she should have said she was taking "proactive action", though if there was any great difference between proactive action and just taking action she was not quite sure what it was. She got out of the car and headed for the door. Less than ten minutes later she was sitting with Kate Bull in her sitting room a cup of tea next to her on a side table and a notebook in her lap.

"So what's all this about?" She asked, getting down to business after a bit of small talk in the kitchen about Jack.

"Well there is not much to say really. I would like to think we could arrange a replacement for Jack. Gosh, what a thing to say, I don't mean to *replace* him, like a broken washing machine. That sounds awful; I hope we will always stay in touch with him."

"I know what you mean and it may not only be possible, it may be possible before too long," said Clare, adding "what about William, does he have the same view?"

"Yes, of course, it would need to be a joint decision, but after all these years I know exactly what he will say. I'll talk to him tonight. This seems to be going faster than I thought possible."

"Well, there are things to arrange, of course, but, as you must have gathered, I do have a lad in mind. Not least we would need to see if you all got on. I can't promise anything, of course, but… " Clare left the thought hanging, she had a good feeling about this, Kate and William had a splendid record, not only in terms of the fostering they had done, but also from her point of view as being easy to deal with: practical, down to earth and just right for the job.

CHAPTER TWENTY ONE

Just what I want

Back in Chelmsford as Clare remained confident as she started to sort things out, both in terms of Kate and William and arranging for a first meeting between them and Terry, on the other side of the city centre Gary Hunt was sitting in his office tapping without enthusiasm at his laptop. His most pressing current case was linked to a marital dispute. Jenny Holmes was a career woman in her late thirties convinced that her husband was having an affair. She wanted proof, for the moment at least she seemed to feel Gary Hunt could get it for her and she had the funds to finance it. Hunt was not enjoying the process. The woman's husband worked in the City, in an investment bank, and he had spent a good many afternoons and evenings waiting for him to leave work and following him to see where he went. So far it was only to Liverpool Street Station to catch a train back home. If he had other assignations on the way they had so far proved fruitless. He sometimes met business colleagues for a drink, mostly in groups and mostly all male, he had attended one or two business functions but done nothing suspicious that even looked like an affair in progress. It was all very tedious. It also involved very few expenses that he could inflate to expand the profitability of the task.

A beep on the computer heralded the arrival of an email. Most of Hunt's messages involved email these days, he could remember the days when most of the interesting stuff came in the post, now that only ever seemed to contain bills. A couple of clicks showed that more than one email had arrived since he last checked. Two were just advertising, one from the auction site eBay, ever since he had used that site to sell something they seemed to contact him with suggestions every five minutes. At least this was understandable, he had registered with the site after all, but the other, which also mailed him with monotonous regularity, even though he had clicked a dozen times to block them from doing so, again offered him the opportunity to apply for some sort of business award. He did not kid himself that his business was at the red hot end of entrepreneurship and deleted it again. The third was an enquiry, which read:

> Dear Mr Hunt
>
> I wonder if you can help. My brother died recently and his will leaves something to an old friend. It is not someone I know but I need to try and trace them, he asked me, my brother that is, to deal with his will and I'm not sure how to go about this.
>
> The friend used to live in Danbury, so it seems sensible to retain someone like you who knows the area. His name was James Crawley. I attach a photo, this is from my brother's house and is quite recent, I think. James is the one on the left.

> Perhaps you would let me know how to progress matters with you and what other information would help. Obviously this needs doing as soon as possible, so please contact me if you can help.
> Sincerely. Lee Maitland (my brother was Alexander J Maitland)

That's more like it, thought Hunt, just what I want. He liked missing person assignments; they were specific, but at the same time there was enough that was open ended about them to take up a good bit of time. He found those asking for people to be found had no idea how to go about it or, therefore, how long the process of doing so would take. That always had possibilities in terms of charging both fees and expenses. He well knew, of course, that not all enquiries resulted in business being booked, nevertheless this sounded like a real possibility. It had some urgency, and the costs would doubtless be paid by the estate. Based on the fact that his brother had died, the enquirer might well be old; that helped too he found, easier to pull the wool over their eyes. If the missing friend was old, then the brothers might well be elderly too. Let's hope so, he thought, as he clicked on the attachment to have a look. There was a slight pause then a document opened over his email screen. It was not the photograph of two old friends that he expected, though the person it showed could very well be called old: it was a picture of a skull.

Hunt may not have been the greatest computer expert in the world, but he did know that was not good, not good at all.

"Bugger!" he said the word three times as he stared in shock at the screen, watching as what proved to be a moving image changed just a small amount, morphing in a way that made it look as if the skull had a lopsided smile. Whatever this was it was getting worse he realised, and he dabbed at the mouse pad to try and delete the image, his panic making him ham fisted and slow. After a moment the image disappeared.

It did not bode well and he wondered if he had been in time to stop further damage.

CHAPTER TWENTY TWO

I shall keep an eye on you

Despite all that was going on, and in part in light of the brick throwing incident, Miriam had not forgotten about the question of Jane Wearing and Philip's insistence that "something should be done". The woman had been warned and Miriam thought it was not likely that she had done the damage to the library, at least not in person; if there was a link between her and the damage then there was, she felt, much more chance that it was with her brother. Her so called psychic activities were another matter. Miriam's unofficial action had involved her in a rather different way and she felt that the matter of her "missing teenager", which had been rather left hanging, needed to be concluded. Besides Philip had told her about his encounter with Mrs Wearing in the library, so Miriam knew that the woman was now aware that Philip thought she was a fraud, their meeting in the library must have made that clear beyond any doubt. Thinking that she should aim for a conclusion of some sort to the matter, at the end of her shift she drove to the woman's house, she parked opposite the front entrance and strode up to the door and rang the bell. She kept her finger on it for rather longer than was necessary.

Jane Wearing answered after just a moment and started by going on the defensive.

"I told your colleague, that incident at the library was nothing to do with me" she spoke with seeming conviction.

"That's not why I'm here," Miriam told her. "May I come in for a minute? Your neighbours will be wondering what's going on."

"Well I have to say…" she paused holding the door open with a gap that did not allow Miriam to effect an entry, then relented, "okay, I suppose so." Her resolve to stop entry evaporated and she pulled the door further open and Miriam walked in. She followed the woman into the consultation room and they sat down opposite each other. Miriam said nothing for a long moment, her intention aiming to make the silence feel unnerving. Jane Wearing's face told her she was successful. After an awkward pause, she spoke.

"I wanted to conclude the matter of the missing teenager," Miriam began, watching Jane Wearing's face brighten at what she seemed to interpret as a positive start. Miriam was quick to dissolution her.

"You know Mr Marchington thinks you are a fraud?" She waited for a reply, adding when none came, "I know about your meeting in the library." This got a brief reaction.

"Mm. Yes."

For a moment it looked as if she had more to say about the verdict Philip had delivered, but she just cast her eyes down and said nothing further.

"Well, I must tell you I'm not impressed either, indeed I have to agree with Mr Marchington. I have to say that I too am utterly convinced that you are a fraud. My session with you gave no impression of your having any special gift or insight, and I only arranged that because I knew you were leading Mary Donaldson on – you remember the lady who sprayed you with paint – taking her money and doing nothing more than persuading her to book another session. I just wanted to see for myself."

Jane Wearing looked cowed, but she did her best to resist all that was implied.

"That's not true, I have a gift … I help people."

"Are you able to help young Stacy?" Miriam posed the question referring back to her supposed missing teenager.

"Well, not yet, I admit, but I could see her, I think she's alive and…" Miriam interrupted.

"She's not alive. She's not dead either, I invented her, the girl doesn't exist at all, and that jacket you focused on belongs to another teenager, a boy. Not very perceptive are you? Not perceptive at all in fact, I would suggest. I just needed to see for myself. I needed proof." She emphasised the word proof, though knowing full well that she could not mean it in a sense that would apply to legal proceedings. After a brief pause, she added:

"Now the question is... what do we do next?"

"What do you mean, do next?" Mrs Wearing looked fearful, her eyes flicked around the room as if trying to avoid Miriam's gaze. She was faced by a stern member of the local police and had just in effect demonstrated to her that her insight was non-existent, a figment of her imagination. She had let her alto ego carry her away. Miriam paused again as she considered her next words with care. She then continued, her voice firm.

"Well, let's see, shall we? I could arrest you for fraud, or for demanding money under false pretences, or..." She paused again and thought it might be useful to give Philip a part to play as she continued.

"Mr Marchington thinks we should throw the book at you, Mary Donaldson no doubt agrees, she was so upset, she was grieving too and goodness knows how many other people you have tricked and taken money from as well."

Jane Wearing opened her mouth and then closed it again; it appeared she could not, for the moment, think of anything useful to say. Finally, in a soft voice she said:

"Please don't, really I meant no harm. I provide comfort for people."

"I think it's more true to say that you give them false hope and get yourself a useful sum of money into the bargain." Miriam gave her a stern look.

"No… no great amount of money is involved. And I help people, it's true, I do."

"So you say. I suppose we could check about the money through your books and your tax return. It is obvious that you view what you do as a business. You do declare the income you get this way for tax don't you?"

At this point Jane Wearing started to cry, she made no sound, but a tear rolled down her cheek and she fumbled in her handbag for a tissue and then, with a quiet sob and a snuffle, wiped her face. Her demeanour made it seem certain that the tax man had never heard of her.

"Lucky for you, cases like this are very complicated. While in many ways the fraud is obvious, it is difficult to get what a court would regard as definitive proof. Nevertheless, I shall check, I shall keep an eye on you and I may well be back with more questions. In the meantime I want to hear nothing more about your so-called psychic activities, do you understand? No complaints, no comments – no anything more at all."

Her question perhaps seemed rhetorical and Jane Wearing said nothing. But Miriam persisted.

"I want your assurance that there will be no more of this, that I will have no more complainants contacting the police, or with grounds to contact the police. I do not want to have to come here again. What do you say?" There was silence for a moment, not because Jane Wearing was considering arguing, but more because she was stunned by the whole exchange. Miriam's manner made it clear that a reply was expected and at last she spoke up.

"Sorry, yes, alright." The voice was contrite now.

"As I said, I would much rather never come here again, Mrs Wearing. Frankly I have more important things to do. So think on the matter. I am sure you would not like a court case brought against you… or the attendant publicity that inevitably goes with that happening." Miriam lent forward a little, looking straight at her as she sat at the table "Be warned," she said, "and you can tell that brother of yours to watch his step too." She threw in a reference to Gary Hunt just to demonstrate the breadth of her knowledge about all that was going on.

Miriam had told Philip she could not in fact threaten the woman, but she was delighted to see that she was getting pretty close. Jane Wearing looked nonplussed. She cast her eyes down and wrung her hands together in front of her: it appeared that the throwing in of knowledge about her brother was the final straw. Miriam reckoned that the job was done.

"I'll see myself out."

She went to the front door, left leaving it open behind her and returned to the car. As she glanced back she saw Mrs Wearing closing the door, she still looked contrite.

Back home later on she updated the others.

"I really think I had the right effect," she said. "You should have seen her face, I rather wished you could have been there." She aimed the last remark at Philip.

"You must have been very convincing, and scary too, I really believe she will think twice about any more funny business, don't you?" Philip looked pleased as he spoke; he wished so much that he could have seen it.

"I certainly hope so, but I hope you realise just how much out on a limb I went there. Please don't speak about it to a soul. You are sometimes very persuasive you know. I wonder now if I should have done it." Philip looked crestfallen and started to speak, but she added:

"Though I'm not the least bit sorry that I did. And I don't think she will be holding any more consultations any time soon."

"I hope you are right and thank you, I hope I didn't push too hard for something to be done." Miriam was becoming more used to his tendency to get the bit between his teeth about things he felt strongly about, but decided enough was enough and moved them on.

"Come on, we need to eat. Besides how are things going next door?"

Philip smiled as Mac and Poy began to update her on their progress. He worried a little that he might have encouraged her to go too far, he did not want her getting into any trouble after all, but he regarded what they had done as a job well done, and the way Miriam had dealt with things today had been superb; she hadn't half entered into the spirit of the thing once she had decided to get involved. He would now be able to say something to Mary Donaldson next time he saw her; not a blow by blow account of course, but enough to make her feel better. He hadn't quite promised, but he had rather implied to her that he would get something done. This would do he thought, this would do very well.

Indeed a few days later he sat with Mary Donaldson at the table area in the library.

"I can't say very much, I can't say anything at all really, and actually bringing the woman to court is really not an option, you know, there being no clear evidence and so on. But take it from me she has had the frighteners put on her good and proper. Let's just say that it was made very clear to her that the authorities are all too well aware that she's a fraud and that she is being watched. Yes, let's just say she now feels unable to continue with her little scheme and there should be no one else caught up like you were."

"Well, it was others I worried about, as you know, I have learnt from the experience I suppose and it's just good to know she has been brought up short, as it were. I won't ask questions and I'll tell no one. Whatever you and that Sergeant of yours have done, thank you so much for your help." She gave him a broad smile, adding: "And I'll try to limit our conversations to library matters in future, now what would you recommend for me to read today, do you think?"

CHAPTER TWENTY THREE

Just a quiet evening in

"Miriam will be home soon," Philip told Terry. "Supper when she's back, okay?"

"Sure," Terry replied adding "Can I use my laptop in the living room?" Philip had noticed that at present Terry seemed to like to have people around and that, unlike many teenagers he did not hide himself away in his room for hours on end. But he seemed to find what might be called a more public environment provided some distraction and that it stopped him brooding; whatever it was Philip was pleased to agree, saying that he had some things to do at the small bureau in the living room.

"Just a quiet evening in for us all," he said, sitting down at his desk in the corner of the room and switching on his own computer. He had promised Mac he would update the estate agent on their progress and the likely date when painting would be finished and the house could then welcome prospective buyers.

As they began to settle to their respective tasks there was a sudden loud crash just behind them. They both turned, startled: Terry, who had been up to his room to get his laptop, was returning through the door of the room as it happened, Philip was sitting at his small desk. It took both of them a mere second or two to realise that something had broken the window from outside the house.

As luck would have it the curtains had been drawn as evening drew in and what proved to be a brick had had its progress slowed on entry but it had still made it into the room and rolled a few feet across the carpet as glass tinkled down below the window. For a moment they were both stunned, saying and doing nothing, then Philip jumped up to see what had been thrown, kneeling on the floor to get hold of it, and offering a loud "Bloody Hell" to the room. It was a normal house brick, with a note attached to it by two jumbo-sized elastic bands. As he thought to himself that this happening looked like nothing more than something from a cheap and clichéd television show, he also linked it in his mind to the events at the library. Mindless vandalism or whatever it was seemed to be spreading and to have his name on it. He realised he should be worrying about, well various things, but right at that moment about Terry, whose temporary safe house must have seemed as if it was being turned into something akin to a war zone.

But as he looked up and around the room he saw that the boy had vanished. Then, a few moments later, a car drove past and, from the sound it made, he realised that the front door was standing open. Terry must have gone outside into the road; had he run out in panic or what he wondered? But he pulled himself together fast, got up from the floor and set off after him.

"Terry," he called, then raising his voice to a shout as he got outside "Terry!" As he arrived at the front gate and was able to see along the road he set off to the right, breaking into a run as Terry's shout of "Here" sounded loud and clear and indicated in which direction he had gone.

Terry had been as shocked as Philip by the arrival of the brick. It was not quite the event you expected after a busy day at school and just when you are in the process of starting up your computer. He had put the machine down on a small side table a moment before and was looking for the electric socket, a process that reminded him that but a short time ago he had been without electricity. But he recovered his wits in a moment: a something thrown through the window meant a something thrower was outside in the road. He dropped the lead for his computer and was on the move in a flash, gone in chase of the window breaker.

Miriam always defined a split second as the amount of time it took between someone seeing a police officer outside their front door and assuming it meant bad news. All too often, of course, it did. Terry perhaps redefined the term; he was out of the front door in the blink of an eye. It seemed clear that whoever had done this was not going to hang about, they would be intent on getting away fast – and unseen, but they had, he reckoned, acted without taking into account a fleet footed teenager, perhaps rather anticipating slower moving adults settled in comfort around the television inside the house. As he went through the gate, which stood open, still with no clear idea of what he was going to do, just identify whoever it was perhaps or get a car registration number, he saw a figure quite close, maybe 20 or 30 yards down the road. The figure was dressed in black and wearing both soft shoes and a hat, but they were not far ahead and neither were they, by Terry's standards, moving very fast. Perhaps hearing Philip and himself shouting the figure glanced behind them and, seeing Terry apparently in pursuit, increased their pace. He assumed they were heading for a car. As Terry broke into a run, the figure glanced back again and he got a glint of spectacles in the glow of the street lights. The shadows made it difficult to make out exactly the kind of person it was. They both increased their pace.

Almost at once Terry realised he could catch up. Again he continued with no great thought about the possible danger, maybe the attacker was armed, but Health and Safety risk assessment was not a concept that featured in Terry's lexicon with any great strength. At the present moment all he thought about was that he could catch them. He closed the distance between them and, still without any clear plan, flung himself forward at the figure just before they reached the corner of the road. Grabbing their shoulders, Terry fell on top of them and pulled them both sideways so that they fell as one across a hedge at the boundary of the house at that moment alongside them. It slowed their progress with a shuddering jerk, supported them for a moment then, under the combined weight of two figures, and amidst the crack of breaking branches, they sagged through it to the ground. Both chased and chaser let out a puff of air as their fall concluded.

"Okay Terry, I'm here," Philip called out as he pulled up just behind them a moment later. Terry sat firm, straddling the figure's back, but glanced round at Philip and then pulled off the figure's hat. What was a tight bun of hair appeared and began to unravel as the figure turned its head towards its captor. Somehow both Terry and Philip had assumed it had to be a man. But they were both wrong - it was a woman, her eyes flashing with anger behind ultra-modern spectacles.

Philip did a double take. He struggled to believe his eyes, but he was not mistaken. He knew who it was.

"Froby!" he almost shouted, "it's… it's bloody well Froby." Even in the circumstances it seemed wrong to use her nickname, so he followed up his comment with "Miss Frobisher, what on earth?"

Then recovering his composure he went on, addressing Terry. "We need to phone the police, but my phone's back in the house."

"No problem. Mine's here" Terry reached into his pocket and passed it behind him.

"You stay put." Philip said to Terry, then dialled the number, thinking that, here at least, it was lucky that no teenage boy would ever be without his phone, not even for a single minute, and still amazed to find Froby had been the brick thrower. He knew he had got her moved on from her job, well in part he had, but she had never said a word about it; indeed he had fondly imagined that she knew nothing of his role in the proceedings. Now he wondered: was this some form of revenge?

"Sit tight Terry," he said once the call was made. "They are on the way." Froby wriggled a little, seemed to discover that she couldn't move and said nothing. Her silence continued despite

Philip posing a barrage of questions. With no replies forthcoming he gave up; he and Terry appeared to have made a citizen's arrest.

When Miriam returned home from a busy late shift she found she had a crime report to fill out, or rather to hear about, as the immediate processes were by then all in hand.

"I can't leave you two alone for a moment," she said, adding some reservations about Terry's have a go action.

"It might have been a man, he might have had a knife or something," she said giving him a stern look, but she then went on to commend Terry for his quick thinking, and added "anyway it worked out okay, so well done you."

"I'm pleased if I helped, you've been very good to me. I guess we made a citizens' arrest, is that right Mr M?"

"Well, I suppose it is." Miriam followed Philip's answer with another comment.

"But that doesn't negate what I've said about the dangers of having a go, right?"

"Okay, but it still felt good," he ended.

Philip turned and swept up glass from below the living room window and then made a phone call to start the process of getting the window secured. Miriam had given him the number of an emergency service that would attend at short notice in the morning to secure the house. There was not much that could be done overnight, but he managed to cut up a couple of cardboard boxes to stick over the hole in the window and stop the cold from getting in to some extent.

After all the excitement it was a take-way meal for supper, eaten amidst a replay of the incident and with Philip repeating in various ways his incredulity at how Froby could have been so upset about things at the library as to take this sort of action.

"Mindless vandalism, I deal with so much of it" said Miriam later as she turned out the bedside lamp, "but I don't really expect it at home or from someone like that."

"Maybe," said Philip "but there is also a certain psychic and her detective friend who have a grudge against me of late. And look at what happened with the damage at the library, do you think there is any connection?"

"Did Froby ever give any indications of having psychic power?" Miriam said laughing. "You've always said she was a witch!"

"Well no, I never did see her broomstick and I hate to think what it would have been like when she was in charge of the library if she had had some sort of superpower. She wouldn't have used it for good, that's for sure. Perhaps it is just a coincidence."

"Anyway leave it for tonight, and well done again to Terry, though I hope he listened to me about need to be careful, not every have-a-go situation ends so well you know. Now I think it's time for sleep."

Just a little time later Philip sat bolt upright in bed and put on the light on his side table.

"There was a note," he said swinging his legs out of the bed. "Tied to the brick, how can I have forgotten? I'll get it." Miriam groaned.

"I was just dozing off," she said. Philip had tossed the brick aside when he had run out of the house and it had then, with all that followed, slipped his mind. A quick return to the living room and he was back in bed clutching a small sheet of paper and reading it out loud to Miriam. The typed words said: "Leave her alone or the spirits will be the least of your worries." It seemed there was no coincidence after all, Froby had to be in some way linked to Jane Wearing.

"But what has Froby to do with all this? I thought she was just upset about her position at the library. I wonder…" Miriam cut him off.

"Enough, please, enough for now" she said eyes tight shut. "In the morning, in the morning."

CHAPTER TWENTY FOUR

A useless detective

Gary Hunt was not happy. He had spent a cold evening following Jenny Holmes' husband when he left his office only to find he went to a dinner at a smart livery company in the city. Doubtless some banking world do. He had no invitation, of course, and he could not have looked less like a banker either; he tried, but they wouldn't let him in, so he had lingered miserable and shivering on the street outside while his quarry wined and dined in warm comfort. When the do ended as his man emerged he followed again, but he then went straight to Liverpool Street Station and got a train back home. Wasted time, thought Hunt, who was beginning to doubt that there was any kind of affair in progress at all, just a suspicious wife and a workaholic husband, though he consoled himself with the thought that the evening did mean he could add a little more to the fees and expenses of the case.

Following his miserable evening, he was late arriving at his office in the morning and did so in a foul mood. He slung his coat over a chair, clicked the kettle on and paced the room while it seemed to take for ever to boil. He made himself a strong mug of coffee, took a sip and then sat down at his desk. Almost at once he thought of the spam enquiry he had received at the end of the previous day and began to worry about his computer. It could have contained some sort of virus. He sipped at his coffee while the machine booted up and then went straight to open his email account. There was nothing new, the offending item was still at the head of his In box list of incoming messages. He had deleted the attachment, but not the email. He did so, wondering why he had not done it the previous day. Anyway it was all gone now. Everything else seemed to be okay, he opened the file in which he was collecting notes and noting expenses on the Jenny Holmes case and that worked fine. He entered a note about the previous evening and his costs and heaved a sigh of relief. Maybe all was well.

Then a ping indicated a new incoming message. Maybe another enquiry, think positive he thought, noting that the address it came from meant nothing to him. But no, the skull was there again; there seemed to be more going on. The skull filled the page in the space for the main message and was overlaid by the words: *Suggest you check your web site and Facebook page.* He cursed under his breath. He cursed out loud, ending his f-ing and blinding speaking out loud with:

"What the hell is going on?"

As he spoke he clicked into Google and his favourites selecting to go into his web site. He was not an expert at this sort of thing, he had paid a small local company to set up his site. It was simple enough, just sufficient information to spell out the kind of thing he did, make him sound professional and make it clear and easy for people to contact him. He was also not very good at keeping the site up to date, he always meant to do something about it and always seemed to find an excuse. So, he had not looked at it for quite a while. He clicked it open.

He was appalled. The neat list of services, each tabbed so that potential clients could find out more about the exact services he offered, had vanished. So too had the flattering but ten year old photo of himself sitting at his desk he had chosen to display, the desk so tidy that it might not have been his; the piles of paper had been moved out of sight to the floor while it was taken. In their place was the skull from the emails to him, this time sporting not a smile but a scowl, written across it were the words:

> Sod off, I'm the last person you would want to employ.
> Signed: Gary Hunt, useless detective.
>
> P.S. If you are still not sure check my Facebook page.

The P.S. was followed by a link. Hesitating a moment or so, he decided he had to see that too and clicked on it. He knew it wouldn't be good, but he could not stop himself from looking. His latest posting, not made by himself of course, was as damning as the first message, this time the picture behind the text was of a crystal ball. The words said:

> Because I am a useless detective, I outsource my cases to a psychic, Jane Wearing, and she's a fraud. So unless you believe contact with a ghost can solve your problem, sod off and don't contact either of us.
> Signed: Gary Hunt, the useless detective

Hunt was not a great Facebook user, though work made it necessary to consult the site sometimes, but he could see that a number of people had already clicked to say they liked it. He didn't kid himself. The fact that they had done so was not flattering, rather it meant the message was spreading. He also noticed that a number of users had added a comment. With rising trepidation he clicked again and found that the first comment said:

What a tosser!

The next said:

Certainly can't solve his own problems

He did not read on, sure that anything more would be similar, just clicked to close the page and turned away. He had some idea of how fast and how far such things could spread online and also realised that he had no idea at all how to fix it. He would have to see what the I.T. guy at the company who had set up the web site could do. He looked up the number, but made another call first.

"Jane, it's Gary. We have a problem." His sister had answered on the first ring and he spoke without preamble.

"Well hello to you too, what's this about then?" Mrs Wearing was well used to her brother's surly manner.

Hunt spelt out the details of what he had just discovered and ended by saying:
"If you have a Facebook account, you might want to check it out. If that's been hacked then I think you should just delete the account."

"How dare they? This is outrageous," Mrs Wearing's voice shook as she spoke "It has to be that Marchington man, though I'd have thought it unlikely that a librarian would be a hacker. We must do something about it. Right?"

"I'll get it fixed. I'm calling the computer guy as soon as we've finished," said Hunt.

"No, no I mean we should report it… to… the… police." Even as she spoke the full implications of what she was saying dawned on her. She had had more than enough of the police of late, the very last thing she wanted was the police taking an interest in her work again, what was it that police sergeant had said about keeping an eye on her? No, she thought, no police.

"Wait a minute, no, we can't. You know we can't. I don't want the police poking into my business again in any way and I doubt you do either. Call the computer man and get it sorted. We'll just have to hope it was a one off, if it was the librarian, then I don't expect he wants to spend his life doing that, he's made his point, he'll leave it. Well, I hope he will."

"Alright," Hunt found himself agreeing. "I suppose we'll just have to see. Leave it for now. I'll call the computer man. Talk later." He put the phone down, leaving his sister thinking that the situation might be dire, but he had no reason to be so surly with her about it.

"Goodbye would've been nice," she said to herself and she replaced the receiver.

Hunt made his call to his computer consultant and agreed, given the situation, to pay a premium rate to get the problem looked at without delay, and someone arrived at his office later in the morning as promised. They spent four hours sitting at the corner table poring over Hunt's laptop. At the end of that time they pronounced all was well again, Hunt didn't ask about the detail of what they had done, but looked at the screen while they displayed his reconstituted web site and Facebook page, which now appeared to be back as they were originally.

"Shouldn't happen again. Well actually it can't happen again now, not now it's fixed right," said computer man, whose name he had said was Malcolm. To Hunt's eyes he looked about twelve years old and as if he should still be at school rather than out in the world of work. He was grateful for the work done, but resented the fact that Malcolm had been unable to resist punctuating his four hours in the office with a series of disparaging remarks about Hunt's lack of computer skills; it was clear he regarded him as some sort of technophobic sub-species. Every comment commenced with a comment beginning with words something like: "Of course, if you had only…" or "I would have thought everyone knew…" and a catalogue of things Hunt should or should not have done, together with the clear implication that it was all his own fault. At one point he had said:

"Of course there's no way of knowing how far this has gone, social media is almost infinite these days, you know. I wouldn't be surprised if Twitter users found it hilarious, it's probably all over that too, hey, there's probably people chuckling at it as far away as China - do you want me to look?" Twitter was a mystery to Hunt and he declined the offer.

"Just sort it so that this kind of thing can't happen again," he said, glowering at Malcolm's back and thinking that, for him at least, it was the very opposite of hilarious; he could not wait for the guy to finish and leave. He just wanted to forget the whole thing. At last Malcolm did finish and left. Hunt heaved a sigh, he just hoped all would be well now and that there were some people left in the world who had not seen the fiasco and might still hire his services. He found the fact that this had happened to be bad enough, the fact that recent events had probably both caused what had happened and now in effect prevented him from doing anything about it brought his frustration to a new level.

As he resolved to put the whole incident behind him the door opened and Steve walked in. An occasional, yet regular, visitor, he was one of the men Philip had encountered on the stairs after his visit to Hunt's office and he had been right, Philip had suspected he had witnessed something shady and his best guess had been that it was about drugs. A few years back, Hunt had been retained to find a missing teenager by the boy's parents. He found him too, living in a squat in Colchester and high on drugs. It was a job well done, the boy had been found in time for steps to be taken to turn his life round; his parents had expressed extreme gratitude. But there was a side effect. During his investigations Hunt had crossed paths with certain unsavoury people in the world of drugs, seen an opportunity and, rather than reporting them, created a role for himself. Steve was lank-haired and in his mid-twenties, he was so skinny it appeared that eating was not much of a priority in his life. He shrugged off a grubby anorak that looked two sizes too large for him and dumped it on one of the chairs as he said without preliminaries:

"Got the next batch have you?"

Hunt knew he was not one for small talk, he nodded and turned to the cupboard beside his desk and removed a small, package, wrapped tight and held closed with brown parcel tape, from it. Their arrangement was well practiced and as he turned back towards Steve he found him holding out a bundle of bank notes that made it look as if his day was about to get a bit better.

It wasn't.

At that moment there was the sound of heavy footsteps on the stairs and, without knocking, someone opened the door. It was the police: two of them in fact, a constable and a man in a suit who stood blocking the doorway and announced himself as a CID officer. He gave Hunt a brief flash of a badge.

When Philip had visited Hunt and had then described his visit to Miriam later, he had mentioned the men on the stairs and his suspicion that they were involved in drugs. As the saga of Hunt, his sister and then his visit to the library had progressed, Miriam had concluded that in all likelihood this was a man involved in activities in which the police might well take an interest. She had filed a routine note about it, which was passed to Chelmsford CID, and thought no more about it; it was outside her area of operation. Thereafter it was just a coincidence, in a bid to enhance their work combatting drug dealing in Chelmsford a CID officer had decided to make a call on Hunt; it was fortuitous that he had picked a good moment. Hunt's day had not had a good start.

"Now, what exactly might be going on here, Sir?" The officer asked his question with exaggerated politeness and Hunt's day took a further turn for the worse.

"Let's have a look at that package shall we. Constable." Both men's hearts sank as the uniformed constable moved forward with his hand held out.

It would be a while before Miriam caught up with this development and told Philip about it all.

"I passed on what you said about those guys at Hunt's office" she told him "CID decided to check him out and, do you know what? They arrived at his door to find a deal in progress right in front of them. A real stroke of luck, I almost feel sorry for the man. It doesn't look like he had any very major role in drugs dealing, but he may well be a link in a chain that leads to bigger fish and that might well prove useful. Anyway they arrested him. And do you know what else? He insisted on filing a complaint amidst all this, it seems someone had just hacked his computer, there were all sorts of messages flying round the ether saying what a useless detective he is. I can't imagine much will be done about that."

When he had heard all this Philp had only a single comment.

"You know when he came asking for me in the library that day, well, when Margaret came to get me she said something about being sure he was 'not a nice man'. So none of that surprises me, and frankly I'd say he deserves everything he gets. Margaret's instincts were spot on, I must tell her." They both hoped that they would hear no more about Hunt. Philip changed the subject.

"Speaking of the library, I had yet another of those 'countdown' cards yesterday. There's still nothing to indicate who they are from or what they are about. It's sooo annoying;

disproportionately so. I mean all the staff know about it, yet none of us have seen anything."

"I told you," said Miriam grinning, "it's signalling the end of the world."

"No it's not. Who would know? The only psychic I know is the Wearing woman and she's a fraud. I bet she couldn't predict lightning in a thunder storm."

Miriam told him not to worry adding: "If it's not the end of the world, I'm sure it will become clear soon. Maybe number ten will explain all, that's a nice round number." Philip shrugged. He had more important things to do and he put both cards and Hunt out of his mind. But Hunt at least would crop up again before too long.

CHAPTER TWENTY FIVE

It got a bit out of hand

Terry was excited and also felt somewhat apprehensive. After all that had happened to him over the last few weeks, today was going to be a very important one for him.

In fact a great deal had been made to happen in a short time since he had at last been made to speak out about his circumstances and Clare Townsend had become involved in his life.

"She's an absolute star," he told Jackson, who continued to be a great support and was always asking how things were going. "Like she's got to fix things for me and I don't really understand the complications, but I know there's lots, yet she's always, well, just friendly I suppose. I like her. Anyone with problems needs a Clare, that's for sure."

Amongst the complications had been first a post mortem and then a funeral. The first, made mandatory in light of the manner of Mrs Walsh's death, was in the background, no one involved wanted to think about it, no one mentioned it. Once done, the verdict was clear: it had been suicide, no surprise there then. Terry has not been given much detail along the way, but once it was done and the verdict given Clare told him it was all over:

"There's a death certificate for your mum now, the funeral can go ahead. Soon all this will be behind you, I don't mean forgotten, I'm sure you will never forget your mum and I'm sure you will always have good memories of her too. But you'll have a new stage of your life starting soon. Something to look forward to. Okay?"

"Yeah." Terry was still not very talkative, but he did draw some comfort from her update.

In due course, Clare had also talked to Terry about funeral arrangements. It was to be a cremation and that meant a simple service. Terry had not been brought up as a churchgoer and had no idea about hymns, services and so on, though it was clear that he recognised the memorial nature of the occasion, even though he had never attended a funeral in the past. Clare felt a bit out of her depth with this too. But she managed to have a word with the Chaplain at Farleigh Hospice, she had visited there to check out the counselling scheme they ran for children who had been bereaved. She was able to make some suggestions and she passed her thought on to Philip who had then briefed the crematorium.

The day of the funeral had been a miserable one: cold, wet and windy, the British winter at its typical worst. Nevertheless it had been done, it had passed and Terry felt better for that. Clare went with him, Philip and Miriam attended and so did Mac and Poy. A number of Mrs Walsh's friends came too, including some from her old work place, as did a surprising number of fellow pupils and parents from Terry's class. That was down in large part to

Jackson, who had put the word round and encouraged their friends to attend. It was a low key but satisfactory occasion and Philip and others all hoped that it being over would make things just a little easier for Terry to move on. To begin with, when the true nature of his mother's disappearance was discovered, he had been quiet, withdrawn, his first reaction shock and worry. Now, with some of the worry subsiding, at least a little bit, his sadness showed more and Philip and Jackson had both had moments with him when he got quite tearful, although he was of an age where he felt that should be fought against and tried hard to keep himself in check.

And moving on he was. Clare had been working hard at arrangements and, in due course, everything was set for Terry to be fostered by William and Kate Bull. They too had attended the funeral. Clare knew them pretty well, of course, and she was sure that Terry would be well cared for by them. She knew they had been excellent parents to others. But it would be good if they hit it off, them and Terry, and Jack too for that matter; he was in Germany at present but he was certain to visit his old home on occasion; he'd promised. He and Kate Bull had exchanged some light-hearted emails about how his old room had been 'rented out already'. He knew there would always be a place there for him as long as he wanted. The kind of situation Terry was in was always difficult. Any child faced with potential new foster parents found the prospect daunting, a feeling reinforced because the opportunity for them all to spend time together had so far been limited. In this case there was an urgency and a cut off time when Philip and Miriam went on holiday. Clare did not want Terry to have a double move moving again to bridge a gap, and going on to some other temporary arrangement with people he did not know, so she had been hustling things along and now, much to her satisfaction, it looked as if everything was set.

Terry had met the Bull's a number of times. He was pleased about the location. He would still be in Maldon, near all his friends, and could still walk to school, albeit from the opposite direction. All that was fortuitous, and Clare remained delighted at the coincidence of Kate Bull's call coming at just the right moment. She had had to juggle with procedure a little, had missed another H.R. meeting and offloaded another case to a colleague to make time, but she had got it sorted and in the circumstances – a known foster family, a bereaved child and Terry's age (it always being more difficult to place older children) – she was content a good arrangement had been made all round. The one downside was that requests from H.R for her to attend yet another meeting had got more insistent; but she could live with that. All Terry's things, in fact everything he wanted from the flat, had been got together and taken out of the flat. There was thus a couple of suitcases and a pile of boxes in Philip and Miriam's front hall. There was little more for him. The flat had been rented. Mrs Walsh had been struggling with money and had had no savings. Terry might get a few hundred pounds at most when matters were completed and the flat cleared. The latter meant the return of a deposit. Clare hadn't said as much, but she rather felt that the new arrangement represented a step up for Terry, the Bulls were well able to look after him, William Bull was solicitor at a large London firm and was, Clare presumed, on a good salary.

At the weekend, a week or so before they were all due to go to Thailand, a time had been set for Terry to move on and Philip was getting him organised; or he was trying to do so. He felt Terry's stay with them had been satisfactory, it had been no great inconvenience to himself or Miriam, Terry was a nice lad and he felt that he had gone out of his way to be an easy guest.

"Are you all set?" Philip asked. "It won't be long until the Bulls are here, you know." There was no response. Terry was sitting on a sofa in the living room with his laptop open on his knee. Philip repeated his question.

"Are you all ready?" Still no response.

Just how many miles away are you?" Philip moved closer, addressing the remark to the back of Terry's head as he moved to stand close behind him. As Terry turned his head, Philip caught sight of what was on the screen just as Terry closed the lid. But he did see one thing that registered: the name Gary Hunt.

"What are you looking at about that detective character?" This question too was received by silence, but not just because Terry was miles away, he wasn't any longer, more because he now wished he could be miles away. At last he spoke:
"Nothing, really, it's just…" his voice tailed off, and as Philip heard the evasion in his tone the penny dropped.

"It was you wasn't it? He said. "It was, it must have been. You attacked that man's computer systems, how on earth…?" Philip found it difficult to imagine Terry being able to do such a thing, yet from everything he read he was aware that the level of expertise of many a teenager on computers was way beyond his own, and that it was almost certain that Terry's went into areas about which he know nothing. He remembered reading about teenagers arrested for major hacking exploits. After a moment Terry spoke up:
"It was a school project," he said, at which Philip interrupted at once:

"How can something like that be a school project?" His tone reflected his incredulity.

"Well, I mean it was going to be a school project, we… I…" Again Terry paused as he realised he was in danger of getting Jackson into trouble too as they had worked in tandem on the project.

"It got a bit out of hand, I guess, I just wanted to help, you've been good to me, you and Miriam, and anyway he was an absolute sh… he was not very nice. I thought he was the vandal and wanted to help. I thought it might put him off. Anyway it wasn't that difficult, his systems were wide open." The way he said the last phrase seeming to indicate that the man had brought it on himself.

Philip was not sure what that meant, though, if it had been easy, he was relieved to learn that Terry's expertise was not therefore set at a level that might have him hacking into the CIA's computers the very next week. He made a rapid decision. He did not doubt Terry's good intention and he knew too that it was all too possible to get carried away in terms of what could be done on a computer. Sexting was a good example. He had no idea why anyone would want of send messages or post things, like nude photographs, online that would come back and bite them as it were, but if the media was to be believed, a huge number of people did so; many of them young. Besides, after all his recent traumas, he very much wanted today to be a good one for Terry.

"Do you think it went too far?" he posed the question to a now wary Terry.

"I suppose…"

"I suppose so too. But I guess I understand. In a way anyway. But it's really not a suitable school project is it?"

"No, we… I've been working on something else now." Philip noted the "we" but said nothing.

"Good, I should think so. Well I don't suppose any great investigation will be done, Hunt's not really in any position to insist on that now, I think. Nevertheless I suggest you delete anything at all about it that's saved on your machine, right… do you promise?"

"It can't be traced." Terry realised that that was not what Philip wanted to hear and changed tack: "Yes, alright. I will. Promise. Are you going to say anything about it? Please don't." Philip guessed he meant say something to Miriam.

"No. I won't. Though I might change my mind if I hear you have been up to anything else in that direction. It's been good to have you here Terry, I hope we have been able to help and I certainly don't want your visit to end on a sour note. Let's just forget it. That okay?"

"Yes, thanks, thanks." Terry heaved a silent and invisible sigh of relief and the exchange was ended as the doorbell rang. Mac and Poy had arrived to see Terry off. Almost before they were inside, and shedding their coats, the doorbell rang again.

After various goodbyes and good wishes, Terry's possessions were loaded in the Bull's car. Mac called him over and handed him an envelope.

"That's the money my mother set aside for you, sixty five pound, remember. You should have it, she wanted you to."

"Right, thanks so much," Terry grinned his appreciation and climbed into the back of the car and he set off with William Bull and Clare to his new home and a waiting Kate Bull, whose slight anxiety had prompted her to check what would now be Terry's room for the umpteenth time.

"Keep in touch," said Philip as he shut the car door. "Let us know how you're doing and say hello if you are in the library."

Terry raised his hand behind the glass as the car pulled away to a chorus of goodbyes, waving hands and shouted good wishes. For Terry a new chapter was under way, one that would include new experiences of which he was as yet unaware.

"Right," said Miriam bringing them all back to earth. "Who's for a cuppa, it's only a few days now until we all go to the airport and you two have a house to finish sorting."

CHAPTER TWENTY SIX

I hope it will be home

Following the exposure of the identity of the window breaker there was one more unexplained loose end to clear up. Miriam had news from the police station.

"I know you've been puzzling about Froby," Miriam told Philp.

"Well, yes, I certainly thought all the trouble, you know the window and the paint at the library, all went back to Jane Wearing and her brother, that one way or another it was them or commissioned by them. I still can't believe that Froby was so upset about losing her job at the library that she would do such a thing. I didn't think she even knew I had, well, sort of nudged things in the direction of her plans running aground."

"She may well not have known. She may still not know."

"How so, what was going on then, I'm assuming now that you know something, come on, out with it?"

"It's really very simple Jane Wearing was married, she divorced many years back, I imagine her husband couldn't stomach her spiritual shenanigans, I wonder if she predicted the divorce." She giggled at the thought. Philip tried to ignore the comment and tried to get back to the business in hand.

"So she was married, what does that have to do with the price of fish?"

"Sorry, I digress. Her maiden name was Frobisher, she's Froby's younger sister."

"Well I never. That explains it, I guess. I wonder how much it was something they organised together or if Froby just took the law into her own hands as it were. She never spoke of a sister when she was at the library, but then she never talked about anything outside of work. Looking back, none of us there really knew anything about her."

"Mystery solved anyway and nothing to do with you and your Machiavellian sabotage at the library."

"Oh, come on, Machiavellian sabotage is a bit hard. Anyway it is good to have that sorted. What a family, eh, I wonder if Froby thought she was psychic too."

Philip found himself imagining Froby sat at a crystal ball.

There is another loose end: you know I told you that Froby was wandering around the library the other day. We still don't know what she had in mind, but if it was some plan we would have hated I bet that it's stillborn now. We may never know." Miriam laughed.

"No need for more sabotage then. All very satisfactory."

On the other side of Maldon, Terry was inspecting his new home and his new bedroom. It was enormous by comparison with his room in the small flat: not only a bed, but built in wardrobes and cupboards, a decent sized desk and an easy chair as well as an upright one at the desk. There was currently a pile of suitcases and boxes that they had between them carried upstairs.

"This is awesome," he exclaimed and Kate Bull smiled with pleasure; she was a motherly soul but business like about things too. She felt that all her preparations seemed to have worked out well. There was also a smaller room in the house that Jack could sleep in if he visited.

"Right, well I'm not sure about awesome, but I hope you will regard it as home. I hope you've got everything you need, there's a laundry basket in the bathroom for dirty clothes and if you need anything else just ask. Please don't worry about anything, we are delighted to have you here and just want you to be comfortable – and happy. Have a bit of a sort out and come downstairs when you're ready and we'll have a bite of lunch. Oh and one rule – no electronics - phones and so on - at the table, okay?" Terry gave a hurried nod. Given the look of his new home and the ongoing welcome he was getting that was something he decided he could live with. He thought about his unpacking and what would go

where for a moment, but then sat down in the easy chair and sent Jackson a text:
```
All seems good c u Monday tell all
```

An hour later as they ate a snack lunch William Bull had a question.

"We thought we might go out for a meal tonight, you know to sort of celebrate your arrival. Where would you like to go, do you think?"

Terry couldn't remember the last time he had eaten out, McDonalds and such places with friends sometimes, but not with his mother, not with adults. Their budget had not run to things like that. Lack of experience left him uncertain what to say.

"If you'd rather stay in, that's okay," Kate offered, "but we reckoned you deserved a treat."

"It's just… I'm not sure, I never used to do that with Mum so… I don't really know." He paused, wondering how to proceed.

"Do you like Chinese? We can walk from here to the Chinse Buffet at Madison Heights," offered William. "We really just wanted you to choose, you know, on your first day. But what do you think?"

"Yes, I'd like that," said Terry, thinking that initial signs were that Clare had done him a really good turn. With their kind, easy going, yet business like, manner his new foster parents were making what could have been an awkward time as he arrived at and got used to his new home easy. By the time they had finished lunch with both William and Kate telling him about Jack, and doing a very good job of creating a friendly atmosphere he knew it was all going to be okay; he was sure that they wanted the best for him, everything might all be new for a while, and he was sure there would be a few more rules to sort out, but he found many of his fears evaporating.

"What now?" said William. "Is there anything you want to watch on television? Did you have Sky at home?"

Terry shook his head.

"Okay, I'll show you the controls, it's easy enough."

After a pleasant day, a good spread of Chinese food at *Izumi,* and a movie in the evening, Terry lay in his new bed that night and felt better than he had done for many weeks. The sadness was still there and he found himself just a little tearful as he thought about his mother and all that had happened in his life recently. He sniffed loudly and wiped his pyjama sleeve across his face to shift the mood, then he reached for his phone and sent another text.

CHAPTER TWENTY SEVEN

The most important person in the hotel

Bangkok shimmered around them in the heat as their taxi carried them from the airport towards the city. With everything that could be done in Abigail's house at this stage done and with good feedback from Terry about his new home Philip and Miriam had left home feeling good and looking forward to their holiday and the time they would spend with Mac and Poy for part of it.

"Nice to be here again?" Philip enquired as their taxi rocketed along the Expressway towards the city.

"Oh yes, it was a great idea, even if it puts the wedding back a little," said Miriam, watching as they left the main road and at once became embroiled in Bangkok's infamous traffic. They stopped at a traffic light, which seemed to stay set on red for hours rather than minutes, then moved on again, their driver weaving from lane to lane yet somehow remaining unscathed. When Philip and Miriam had visited Thailand for the first time, following up clues that in due course led to them finding Mac at the marina in Phuket, they had spent a day or two in Bangkok before travelling on, sightseeing and well, with what they had now given the delicate description of "delight in oriental setting". It was not something that Philip would forget in a hurry, although if Miriam had taken the lead there, he felt he had topped it by a proposal of marriage on the journey home, now known to them both as "the mad, but right moment".

On the first trip as part of their original sightseeing to the Grand Palace, temples and a huge weekend market where stalls selling everything on earth stretched into the distance, a visit to a hotel was involved. Philip had taken Miriam to see the iconic Oriental Hotel, a place where its history and traditional values still prevailed despite modern times and the modern extensions that had been added to the original building over the years. It was indeed impressive, though Philip had commented that staying there would necessitate spending "a very serious amount of money". Despite that they had enjoyed a drink by the river on its famous terrace; "You can't visit Bangkok and not do this." Philip had insisted. Now they were back in the city of angels as it was called.

Miriam had left all the detailed holiday arrangements to Philip and not even thought about them with so much going on at home while Mac and Poy were visiting. They had flown from Heathrow with them but they had parted company in Bangkok airport where their friends had transited straight onto a domestic flight to Phuket and home. Now, as the taxi turned into smaller streets and slowed still more, Miriam was surprised when she recognised that they were at the Oriental Hotel as their taxi headed up the ramp and stopped outside the main entrance. Once they had got off the expressway and into the city's congested streets, while she had marvelled at the sights and sounds, for instance taking a delight in counting the absurd number of people that could be somehow squeezed onto a single small motorbike, she had not had any very clear idea of where they were going.

"What's this — a burst of extravagance?" she asked. "Or is it just an in and out visit for breakfast?"

"No, bit of a surprise, it's all fixed. We are staying here. My treat." Philip didn't add that he had done a good deal on the rate and it was not quite as expensive as he had originally thought. "I just thought that 'our honeymoon ahead of the wedding' as it were should start in style, and anyway when we move on to Phuket we will stay in a cheap shack and sleep on the beach." He grinned.

"Well, just so that you know, despite this treat I shall be expecting a certain style throughout the whole trip." She paused, adding: "Though I suppose the budget must leave sufficient for a wedding when we get home, you are still thinking about that, aren't you?"

"Of course, but..."

At this point their conversation was curtailed by a uniformed doorman opening the door of the now stationary taxi, Philip handed over some *Baht* to the driver and the doorman began to collect their luggage and see them on their way to check in.

Philip felt he must be looking a bit bedraggled after their long haul flight, but if there were any respectability police in the grand lobby they seemed to pass muster and at the Reception counter they were greeted with due ceremony, had their passport details noted and were issued with room keys.

"I think you'll find the room comfortable," the receptionist assured them with a smile so well qualified to put her into any toothpaste advertisement that Miriam wondered if Philip was flirting with her. She wondered too if one thing not to like about Thailand was the extreme attractiveness of so many of their womenfolk, it seemed very apparent that those chosen to work in hotels were selected, in part at least, for their looks. This one might well have taken a day off from her duties as Miss Thailand just to check them in. A uniformed porter showed them to their room and their luggage arrived a few minutes later. The room looked very much as if they would be comfortable, the many silks and subtle colours created a restful and sumptuous atmosphere. It was clear their stay would prove a real spoil.

"Well done, you," said Miriam. "This is certainly a pretty good start to the trip, thank you. What a view, look, just spectacular." They stood together at the window for a few moments looking out at the river, on which an assortment of boats moved to and fro, before starting to unpack.

There is no easy answer to jet-lag, most people find that the first day after a long haul flight passes in a bit of a daze, but a day spent by the Oriental's pool and a trip along the river to have a drink at the hotel they had stayed in on their last visit – the site of my seduction as Philip put it with a mischievous grin – did a fair job of taking the sting out of it. As the day drew to a close, Philip suggested an early night.

"We need to catch up on our sleep and try to get ourselves firmly onto Thai time," he insisted.

"Are you sure it's sleep you want to catch up on?" Miriam responded. "Or something else to start the holiday?" Philip thought about it for the merest split second before he replied.

"Well, it did all start here, so perhaps something else first, then sleep."

The following morning, they woke much refreshed. Philip had organised breakfast in the room. It arrived on a trolley, laid out in a way that provided another example of the Oriental's perfectionism and attention to detail.

"This is wonderful, what a treat," said Miriam as she sliced into what seemed to be the best pineapple on the planet. "But I can't believe you set an alarm on the second day of our holiday – honeymoon - rather."

Philip ignored the comment and poured more tea. A little later he looked at his watch and jumped up.

"Heavens, look at the time. It's the jet-lag. I almost forgot all about it, Mac and Poy have someone they want us to meet. At 11.30. They said it's really important, I don't want to let them down. Is that okay?"

"I guess so, what's it about?"

"I bet they've arranged a trip of some sort for us, but they said we should dress up for it. I think it will be a bit of a treat so I didn't say anything, but I did pack a smart dress for you. We need to ask for a *Khun* Katai."

They had not yet worked out the business of packing to go away together. In some households one party does it all, in others it is more of a joint effort. For the most part they had packed separately, a case each, and Philip now went to the wardrobe where on the previous evening he had hung a dress of Miriam's which he had packed in his suitcase.

"Oh no!" Miriam exclaimed as she saw it and sounded anguished. "Not that one, that was supposed to be for the wedding."

"Oh dear. I'm so sorry, I just picked what looked smart. It was a last minute thing just before we left. But, come on, chop, chop, we have to go and you shouldn't just wear a t-shirt."

Miriam grumbled a bit, but she did a rapid change and they headed off to the Oriental's palatial lobby.

"They arranged for us to meet in the old wing. This way."

Philip led the way through the passage that connected what was the newer wing of the hotel, now containing the main lobby, to the old and on through into the Author's Lounge, a beautiful space furnished with white wicker chairs and tables and with a double staircase giving access to the special residential suites above. At one end, the lounge, in the direction of the river, seemed to lead through into another room, one at present roped off with a sign saying "Function in progress". As they came to a halt in the middle of the room, Poy appeared accompanied by an elderly Thai lady, elderly but looking spry beyond her years and clothed in impeccable style in Thai silk.

"Good morning. This is *Khun* Katai," said Poy sounding very formal, "she is most important person in hotel."

Philip thought he knew someone else to put first, but he kept quiet, watching as *Khun* Katai greeted them with a wai, a slow raising of her hands as if in prayer in the traditional Thai greeting, while Miriam looked mystified, wondering who this person was and why Mac and Poy had organised for them to meet her. Besides she thought hadn't they flown straight on to Phuket? What was Poy doing here? She thought Philip had been a little odd this morning, springing the meeting on her and even bringing her a dress to act, as he said, as "smart wear". It couldn't be she thought … but just as the penny was about to drop she heard a smiling *Khun* Katai say:

"All is arranged, I am here to welcome you to your wedding. Please come this way."

Miriam felt Philip take her hand in a firm grip and the sound of familiar music beginning to play seemed to remove all possibility of protest. Another member of the hotel staff opened the rope barrier and as they turned the corner into the small Library room alongside the Authors' Lounge she was greeted by more flowers than she had ever seen in one place before and by not only Mac, but also by Philip's sister Pauline, her husband David and their two children. She paused to give them all a quick hug. In effect she had two bridesmaids, Pauline and her daughter Jill, while Philip had Mac briefed to play the part of his best man.

Then as Philip led her towards the front of the room from where the service would be conducted she squeezed his hand hard.

"I had no idea. You bugger!" She whispered.

"That's not quite the reaction I had hoped for," replied Philip also in a whisper, "and that's not a nice word to use of your husband to be, in public too. You know what I tell the kids in the library who use it: 'it's only suitable for describing unruly dogs, rambunctious children and those at Regional Library HQ who interfere in local branch affairs'."

"Oh, shut up, I'll talk to you afterwards. Don't you dare say a single word… well, except 'I do', I guess, I will allow that!"

Philip couldn't help remembering his first marriage service. He and Penny had been happy until her untimely death, but the marriage service itself seemed like something from another age. A conventional church service after a conventional engagement and a gathering afterwards that was, to overuse the word, conventional. It had seemed good at the time. It was fun, it was just right for them starting out together. It had been well suited to the times. To describe this as different was an understatement, it was so very different. Early on in the short time he had known Miriam, they had found themselves travelling the world together, he – a cautious soul for the most part – had amazed himself by proposing to her almost on a whim, though he remained convinced it was right and now he'd followed that by arranging a surprise wedding that was taking place on the other side of the world from their home. The honeymoon before the wedding as they had dubbed this trip was about to change into the honeymoon after the wedding. He might have difficulty believing it, but it was all true and it all seemed so right. Lucky him. He let the fact that the word she had limited him to was, in fact, two words pass and stepped forward towards the next stage of his life. An official organised by *Khun* Katai moved forward to greet them and not so many minutes later they were pronounced man and wife. After a small amount of paperwork and some signatures all was made official.

✷

"I. have. Never. Been. More. Surprised. Somehow even the dress didn't give it away. However did you keep this secret? However did you arrange it, however did you even *know how* to arrange it? And what about consultation? We agreed to make joint decisions about our future life together. And …"

"Give me a chance! First things first … was it a good surprise?" Philip asked.

"Well, I suppose it…"

"Suppose, suppose… was it a good surprise?"

Miriam beamed at him.

"You know it was, it was amazing. Just amazing, but however did you…" Again Philip interrupted her.

"With a little help from my friends, after all we are in a foreign country, it had to be done right and proper, I didn't want us getting home and finding the marriage wasn't valid; you might have found yourself arresting us for impersonating a married couple. *Khun* Katai organises many weddings here, large and small, and it was you who insisted on small, remember, so I knew that was okay. She knew exactly what to do to make it right – and make it official, all Mac had to do was…" This time it was Poy's turn to interrupt.

"Mac, know nothing, not about this. I fix with *Khun* Katai and she fix good … yes?" Following Philip's request and Poy's briefing of *Khun* Katai, Mac had sent Philip her email, laying out the suggested arrangements in meticulous detail, and Philip had checked and confirmed it all. He had been liaising with his sister too, her family were linking their attendance at the wedding to a long overdue holiday with the children.

"She did indeed fix it good, it was a great surprise and a great occasion – simple, dignified and just ideal - thank you all, thank you so very much." Miriam looked round the little group and gave them a broad smile.

She kissed them all in turn. Including *Khun* Katai who took it all in her stride, though having participated in a European-style hug and kiss on the cheek, she stayed close to Miriam for a moment more. She whispered to her.

"I wish you both great happiness. I am sure you be happy. But I think you have secret, maybe even small secret not good idea at this time." She gave Miriam a serene smile, stepped back and *waied* to the little group with due formality before taking her leave and returning to her other duties. She had a disgruntled regular guest to pacify, and must somehow explain to them that because the hotel did in fact have guests other than himself he could not *always* occupy the same suite on every visit. She made her way towards Reception thinking of just how she could put it. While some people may be said to have the tact and diplomacy of a sledgehammer, *Khun* Katai, while her job often called for toughness, had both qualities in spades when necessary. Miriam wondered how she could know, but she was correct, she did have a secret and it was something that remained to be dealt with.

The spell was now broken as Philip's nephew, John, piped up, bringing them all back to earth.

"Uncle Philip have we been good enough? You promised us ice-cream after."

"And beaches," added Jill.

"All in good time," said Philip, "and yes, you've been very good, though there was a moment yesterday when I though Miriam had spotted you in the pool. But it's your Mum and Dad you need to talk to about the beaches. For now we get to eat, a wedding breakfast of sorts, well it must be breakfast time somewhere in the world, though that's just an expression isn't it? We start with a drink… and ice cream for you two. Come on."

They headed for the restaurant at the rear of the hotel and sat overlooking the terrace and the river beyond. They ate just a snack, though the ice creams were to say the least generous. Then they all returned there in the evening when there was the regular splendid and lavish hotel barbeque laid out right beside the river and they sat together at a round table and could watch the lights of the city beyond. The children took some bread from the buffet and fed the huge catfish that came to the surface below the rail round the terrace. Every one of them pronounced it a splendid end to the day. They all headed for bed in good time, still not caught up with the time difference between Thailand and England as much as they would have liked and with the children flagging after a long exciting day, and arranged to meet for breakfast. Meantime Philip and Miriam had a little further celebration on their minds, just the two of them. Over a drink in the hotel's music bar, with a small jazz group playing in the background, they chinked glasses and Miriam smiled a happy smile at Philip who toasted her as Mrs Marchington.

"That was all wonderful. What a day! What a surprise! I still can't really believe it all happened, but I may have said that before. You are quite an organiser when you put your mind to it, but I've a confession to make," she said.

"Oh, what's that?" Philip replied.

"Well, you know your mysterious 'countdown cards' that have appeared pinned up in the library?" Philip nodded, it seemed to him an odd thing to be thinking about in the circumstances but he waited with interest for further explanation.

"Well, it was me," she said, shushing him when he threatened to interrupt, continuing "after a few more postings they were going to declare their purpose and spur you on to arrange a wedding. I didn't really think you were going to neglect it, honest, it was just a bit of fun. But then we fixed the holiday and, well, you beat me to it."

"You wicked… oops, I nearly said bugger. Well, that's a surprise too, how did you do it though? No one ever saw you in the library, much less pinning up the cards."

"Oh, I didn't do that myself, Margaret did the actual posting, she was happy to help."

"The minx, I was never going to spot that, I'd put her in charge of the notice board, after all. I shall have words with her when we get back. So surprises all round. Perhaps we should return to more conventional ways of communicating in future."

"Okay, it's a deal and let me start by saying this. You really do have some very good ideas on occasion," she said "The wedding was all just amazing… I must stop saying that word, and I had no idea; none at all. How could I not have guessed?" Philip smiled back.

"As you said, it must have been my brilliant organisation Mrs Marchington. Well, anyway I'm very pleased you approve, and I'm relieved too. It seemed like a plan with a beginning, a middle and an end, but I wanted it to be right for you as well as a surprise. I must confess I did have a smidgen of doubt about your reaction. So a good idea then. And you know what? I've just had another good idea. Coming up?" He drained his glass, signalling her to do the same.

It seemed that the day's celebrations were not quite over yet.

EPILOGUE

Very good decisions

Sometime the following year…

Mac thought it had been a good decision; more than one good decision in fact. But now it was business as usual, he untied the rope securing the bow of the boat and stepped onto the deck as the craft moved away from the pontoon. At the helm, Poy was in mischievous mood and allowed the boat to accelerate a little as he did so, but timing it just right, he got on board safe and sound even if he had to complete his jump aboard pretty smartly. She flashed him a smile, then called out to their passengers.

"Okay, we go now, take about an hour to the island, then lunch."

The boat glided forward, making its slow and smooth way out of the busy marina, into the main channel and on towards the open sea. It was a beautiful day. The sun shone from a cloudless sky, the wind and sea were just right for the sail, it would allow them to make good progress yet keep all aboard comfortable too.

Soon the noise of the engine, which had been needed to get them clear of the marina, died away, the sails were raised, were at once filled by the wind and they were on their way. They made a good team, Poy continued to man the helm for a while, then drinks were served and the passengers, two couples on holiday together, settled into their seats chatting together as the boat knifed its way through the clear, sparkling water. The wind was sufficient to create an impressive bow wave in the water and an occasional burst of spray reflected in the sun as it hung for a second or so in the air and then sometimes reached the deck. For a few minutes a pair of dolphins were visible humping out of the water alongside as they went towards some unknown rendezvous and the sight drew exclamations from the passengers.

One of those aboard, who had done some sailing in the past, was keen to learn about handling the boat. For Mac this was always a bonus, he loved passing on his sailing skills. After a little while he, having served drinks all round, took over from Poy and began a tutorial for them. First he pointed out the basics, how each sail was controlled, the amount of effort that needed to be applied to turn the boat and an overview of the route they were on towards their island destination, an island which was appearing larger and larger as they went towards it.

"Your turn, let's see how you do." Mac handed over the steering and the course of the boat began to vary as he gave instructions to move the boat tighter into the wind or tack, rather more than he would have done without a pupil, with the various manoeuvers designed to give a real impression of how the boat handled and how best to sail her. She was a larger boat than his pupil was used to but he managed his task well. Mac had no need to intervene.

In due course they were approaching the island, and then, with the sails lowered and the anchor dropped, Poy organised the party ashore and onto the beach, a long unspoiled stretch of white sand experience told her would make their guests feel they were on their own private desert island for a while.

"I'll fix lunch," she said. "Time for swimming, cool down before we eat if you want. There is snorkel equipment in that bag. Help yourself." She pointed at the large canvas bag that lay on the sand. Their guests seemed happy enough with that and all moved towards the sea for a dip as she began to lay out the food, while Mac set up a small barbeque. This was one of their standard offerings, a four or five hour trip out to a nearby small island, time to swim and explore, and time too to appreciate the boat and the sail and have a go at the helm if that was something their guests wanted. Nevertheless it was a trip that they enjoyed too, over the years they had located many different places that made suitable destinations. Today they were on a small island and had sailed round to its far side; they knew that their guests liked it most when the bulk of Phuket Island itself was hidden: it gave them more of a sense of being off the beaten track.

"Lunch ready now," Poy called as Mac's barbequing reached perfection and the group gathered round tucking into the food with gusto and drinking *Singha* beers taken ice cold from the boat's refrigerator.

"These prawns are amazing," Judy one of the guests led the praise amid a chorus of appreciative mmmms.

"Say *Aroy,*" Poy told her, "means delicious." She knew most *farang* found the Thai language very difficult to speak, as it was a tonal language, with many sounds having no equivalent in English and with the same word meaning different things when pronounced in different ways. Despite this, and despite the fact that many visitors to the country, particularly those staying in large resorts, found no real necessity to learn any Thai, Poy always offered a few tips and saw it as part of the experience of sailing with them. The meal over, the guests set off for a long walk along the shore, allowing the crew to pack away the remains of lunch and then relax for a while in the shade. Poy picked a spot with no coconuts lurking as a potential danger in the trees above them. This was a real hazard, coconut palms grow high and she knew that more people around the world are killed by falling coconuts each year than are attacked by sharks, and she always picked their spot for lunch with due diligence.

"Don't want dead customer," she had told Mac once, by way of explanation for insisting on always picking where they ate with care, "might not pay!"

Around them there was no noise other than the soft sound of small waves breaking on the beach and the wind rustling the branches of palms high above them.

"Too hot to walk," offered Poy, who not so many months ago had been complaining of the cold British weather and was pleased to be back in her native land and what she referred to as a 'normal' temperature. Time passed in comfortable chit chat and soon their guests, having dwindled to dots in the distance, returned along the sand with more cold drinks an essential requirement before they moved on.

"Sorry, folks, time to go if we are to have you home in time for supper," said Mac.

"This holiday is just one meal after another," said one of his guests and they all laughed.

"You had good walk," said Poy, "some exercise. No problem."

"Yes, and what a spot, what a great afternoon" said Judy and the others all murmured enthusiastic agreement.

With the lunch things having been stowed while the guests walked, they all waded out to the boat and climbed aboard at the stern. Mac took charge this time. There was no need for the engine here away from the marina and with the anchor raised and the sails deployed they were soon on their way. As everyone found a spot to sit where they were comfortable and contemplated a relaxing voyage back to Phuket, Mac was joined again by his pupil.

"Can I have another go?" he asked, and Mac grinned at him. He had never seen such enthusiasm.

"Well, I think you pretty much know what to do now, don't you. Take us home Terry. *Abigail* is all yours." He moved away from the helm and watched as the young man took control and the beautiful new boat surged ahead. He smiled across at Poy, telling himself that, sometimes at least, he made some good decisions, some very good decisions indeed.

END

Acknowledgements

As with *Long Overdue,* the first novel involving some of the characters depicted here, I have set some of the action described in and around Maldon in north Essex. I know it, love it and live there; most of this book was written looking out over the estuary of the River Blackwater towards which my house faces.

I have, however, taken some small liberties with the geography of the area and more important, there is no direct link here with actual local practices as they may be conducted in the real library and the District Council, which I am sure may vary. In similar manner, I have people populating real places in the town and all such characters are of course fictional.

Thanks are due to a number of people: the members of the writing group to which I belong who encouraged me, my daughter Jacqueline, herself an author, who read and commented on the first draft and, of course, the publisher, Lloyd Bonson, who was supportive throughout and did such an efficient job of turning my manuscript into a finished book

Also from the Author

First Class At Last!
An Antidote to Past Travel Horrors
More Than 1,200 Miles in Extreme Luxury

Fed up with the strenuous process of travel: the slow queues, the delays, the crowds and the extreme discomfort of the average economy airline seat?

Patrick Forsyth decided it was time to do something about this. He arranged a trip designed to be the antidote to the routine travel misery - and booked a trip travelling only first class.

The first challenge was to decide where to go. He decided to fly to Bangkok, stay in the world renowned Oriental Hotel, continue onto Singapore and stay at the equally famous Raffles Hotel. He then travelled in style back to Bangkok on the Eastern and Orient Express, where he spent two nights on what many people regard as the best train ride in the world, and finally concluded his travel at a luxury spa on the beach, to recover.

Along the way, the author meets a rock and roll musician; visits dubious bars and colourful markets; has an encounter with the bodyguards of the Thai Royal Family; and embarks on a boat trip along the River Kwai. This lively, amusing account of luxury travel, highlights what every traveller secretly longs to do - travel in style and grandeur.

> **"...witty and full of facts ..." Essex Life**

> **"... Lively, witty and wry." Select Books**

> **"... it reminded me of Bryson..."**
> **Neal Asher, bestselling author of Gridlinked**

Long Overdue

By his own admission, Philip is living a humdrum life in the Essex coastal town of Maldon.

His new boss at the town library is a pain in the neck, making even the job he loves difficult, and he longs for something to kick start him out of what he admits is a bit of a rut. Soon after a new and unexpected friendship begins he determines to make some changes.

Then one day his routine walk to work has him finding a dead body, involved with the police and feeling he must help his new friend by investigating a mystery from years past.

As events following the death carry him along, an abandoned sailing boat, half a letter and a surprising alliance sees him seeking to unravel the mystery of a missing person.

He quickly realises that dialling the emergency services that spring morning is leading to changes that will affect his life, his job and his future as well as having him travel abroad and make some surprisingly impulsive decisions

"Patrick Forsyth has written many non-fiction books but this is his first novel. It comes with a real ear for dialogue and a pulse-quickening sense of risk. As for Philip, he is a thoroughly well-rounded protagonist for whom you root from the start."
The Good Book Guide

About The Author

Patrick Forsyth is the much published author of many non-fiction books. Many offer guidance to those working in organisations, for example *Successful Time Management* (Kogan Page) is a bestselling title on its subject.

He has also written three light-hearted books of travel writing: *Beguiling Burma* about a river journey through that delightful country, one now ever more in the news as changes occur and many watch anxious to see if the conditions for its people improve. Of this book one reviewer said: *Patrick is a born writer with a clear transparent style, a great eye and plenty of wit ... I was really, really impressed.*

The second travel book is about Thailand and titled *Smile because it happened* and there is also *First class at last!* about a trip on the Eastern & Oriental train that runs through Singapore, Malaysia and Thailand and which, like this book, is also published by Stanhope Books.

Patrick is also author of the humorous book *Empty when half full* (Rethink), a hilarious critique of miscommunication that misleads and **amuses and was praised for its** ... *needle-sharp and witty observations*.

His first novel, *Long Overdue*, remains available from Stanhope Books and elsewhere. On his most recent project he has worked with Lloyd Bonson to produce a book of short stories, *A Great Little Gallimauphry*, which is published by Stanhope Books and sold in aid of Farleigh Hospice (in Chelmsford, Essex).

He lives in Maldon in north Essex and this is his second novel.

Contact invited and is possible via: www.patrickforsyth.com

Other Fiction from Stanhope Books

A Higher Authority – *Barrie Hyde*

A young Oxford graduate with a gift for languages joins MI5 and is then seconded to 'A Higher Authority', an organisation funded through government sources from around the world which nobody would admit to.

Countries have to be seen to be playing it straight, and sometimes can't get at the bad guys. This is where 'The Organisation' comes in.

Our hero is given the code name Jonathan to 'avoid contagion' and trained at an old British Army camp in Kenya, where he meets and falls in love with his Zan, a Chinese colleague.

Catapulted into the world of industrial espionage their mission is to find out from the inside how a company has been able to grow at lightning speed. They find themselves embroiled in kidnapping, murder, drug running and money laundering.

Watermelon Man – *Peter Norman*

Regaining consciousness late at night in a dark alleyway in a strange town, the man realises that he has been mugged and robbed of everything—including his memory!

He begins a journey that turns from a dream into a nightmare as nothing is as he had hoped it would be.

Forced to confront his demons, his problems collapse into a web from which there appears to be no escape . . .

www.stanhopebooks.com
facebook.com/stanhopebooks
Twitter @stanhopebooks

#0001 - 171117 - C0 - 203/127/15 - PB - 9781909893542